Puffin Books

Hero

'This was it, the limit . . . It was fine to think of riding
a mad river in a flood, but this was getting serious.'

Darcy, Pam and Barney. Each very different, each in
danger. Forced together by the rising waters of the
Hawkesbury, as their familiar world is ravaged by
flood. Then, fear and anger give way to blinding
terror . . . But can they survive? And who will be the
hero?

Hero, based on the Sydney flood of 1986 and set in the
outer suburb of Richmond, is another gripping novel
from this award-winning author.

Also by Allan Baillie

Adrift
Little Brother
Riverman
Eagle Island
Megan's Star
Drac and the Gremlin
Mates

Allan Baillie

Hero

Puffin Books

Puffin Books
Penguin Books Australia Ltd
487 Maroondah Highway, PO Box 257
Ringwood, Victoria 3134, Australia
Penguin Books Ltd
Harmondsworth. Middlesex, England
Viking Penguin, A Division of Penguin Books USA Inc.
375 Hudson Street, New York, New York 10014, USA
Penguin Books Canada Limited
10 Alcorn Avenue, Toronto, Ontario, Canada M4V 1E4
Penguin Books (N.Z.) Ltd
182-190 Wairau Road, Auckland 10, New Zealand

First published in Great Britain by Blackie and Son Ltd, 1990
First published by Penguin Books Australia, 1990
Published by Puffin Books, 1991
10 9 8 7 6 5 4 3 2 1

Printed and bound in Australia by the Book Printer, Victoria.

National Library of Australia
Cataloguing-in-Publication data:

Baillie, Allan, 1943-
Hero

ISBN 0 14 034427 6.

I. Title.

A823'.3

To Tanner, for getting her feet wet

The school in the book does not exist, but my deep thanks to the pupils and staff of St Monica's School of Richmond for helping me write the book. And my thanks to the State Emergency Services of New South Wales for their advice.

1

A single drop of water exploded on Pamela Browning's open exercise book. Pam started, sending an HB pencil skittering across her desk, and stared as the water spread over her carefully created map of Europe.

Two hours' work destroyed. Pam throttled the pencil and stopped herself from hurling the exercise book away. Annabel was smiling sugar at her. Pam smiled thinly. They were friends; Annabel could not have seen the mess. Pam lifted her eyes and glared at the high, stained ceiling and dared it to throw another bomb at her.

Miss Rader ran her fingers tiredly over a rough roll of project paper as she shouted above the rain about a king or two, but few could hear, and fewer were trying. Pam was wishing that she was home, on the hill above the river, warm and dry, when she heard the faint sound of the door sliding.

Mr Graham was leaning on the leading edge of the door, looking more like a captain of a sinking ship than a headmaster. Miss Rader shouted on for half a sentence, then noticed the sudden shift of attention, saw Mr Graham and stopped.

The rain roared in to fill the space, exploding against the tiled roof, streaming down the walls, rattling the windows. The worm of water where the ceiling met the outer wall had become a long flat snake, writhing toward the blackboard.

"Mr Graham?" said Miss Rader. But she knew. Everyone knew.

"We'll have to let them go, Dot," Mr Graham said with a nod at the running windows.

Pam thought: Out! Away from everything that stinks and drips.

Miss Rader nodded.

Then Pam glanced casually at the roll of paper under Miss Rader's finger and realized she could not leave. Not yet. She had seen the bright yellow of her project on the Hawkesbury River a century ago. Weeks of chasing up old maps, newspapers, books, even talking to a family that had been here since the river's first recorded flood. It was about to be unveiled.

"The police have just phoned," Mr Graham said. "The bridges are expected to go under."

So much for the unveiling.

"Yes."

What else could she say? The way the rain had fallen over the last twelve hours it was a wonder the Hawkesbury had not already broken its banks. Sydney was sinking.

"I've asked the buses to come to the shelter sheds. Get the kids ready." Mr Graham shrugged and moved away to the next class along the corridor. The school intercom had died of fright in the first wave of rain, warning the school that today was going to be rough.

Miss Rader turned to her desk and absently began to stack her books. "Well, you heard Mr Graham. School's finished for today."

But now the project would be left here, in the dripping water, to be ruined like her map of Europe.

"Beauty!" Darcy Harris, lump of a boy, dull as a tortoise, punched at the air and kicked himself away from his desk.

"Enough, Harris!" Miss Rader shouted down the rain and the growing racket in the room. "Get your bags ready, children. Coats on. Walk—don't run—to the shelter sheds. All right?"

The thirty children rose noisily from their desks, a disturbed nest of wasps. Pam saw Harris grin and strike behind him with a low fist and Barney Stevens stopped abruptly, pain caught in his face. Miss Rader started to call Harris back but changed her mind, too much to worry about.

But Pam looked down at her ruined map and at her very fragile project. "Miss Rader?"

"Yes, Pam?" wearily.

"What about our homework?"

The groan almost stopped the rush to the door. Pam was pointing at the projects rolled on the desk, but no one except an elephant of a girl called Marjorie saw the arm. Annabel stared at Pam in shock and clapped her hand on Violet's shuddering shoulder for dramatic support.

"Oh, yes," said Miss Rader. "All of you can give me three hundred words on Sturt—with a map. To be handed in when we resume school. Whenever that is."

"Thanks heaps, Pam," Barney muttered as he pushed past her.

Harris hadn't been part of the class groan and he wasn't part of the dying protest now. He simply wasn't going to do it.

The children flooded into the corridor, shouting, grabbing at their raincoats, pushing at each other. Then, out, free into the rain.

Pam stayed back for long enough to see Miss Rader place her project and a few others in a cupboard, then followed the others. She was alone. Annabel, Violet and the others in the A-Team had left her, as if they had never known her. She had made a bad mistake, but they would forgive her eventually. They always did.

She walked a few steps from the building and opened her mouth, listening to the crackling roar of the water on the heavy plastic of her hat. The sky was a swirling, tumbling mass of deep purple cloud as she lifted her face to taste the rain, but immediately the rain battered her eyelids painfully shut. She bowed her head for shelter as a gust of scudding wind pushed her hard in the back and she staggered into a puddle.

"Goody Goldilocks!" Suddenly she was surrounded by rain-streaked figures in yellow and red.

"Go away!" she shouted.

" 'What about our homework, Miss?' " Mocking, pushing, almost hitting her on the shoulder.

"Teacher's pet!"

"Whyn'cha lick her shoes?"

A violent shove, a leg behind hers and she was falling into an ocean of stippled black water. For an instant she was lying on the ground and the water was rearing, arching from her with a loud slap, and the legs around her were dancing, scuffling. Then the wave faltered, fell and rushed back, cold fingers up her arms, along her back. She shouted and someone pulled her rainhat over her eyes.

"Hey!" A boy's voice, and there was confusion, a milling of legs and a knee pounded into her ribs. She felt her dress caught and torn.

"All right, then!" Mr Graham, booming against the storm, and she was alone in the puddle.

She pushed her hat to the back of her head, saw Mr Graham striding toward her from the corner of the school, Harris, looking slightly surprised, standing at her feet, Barney offering her his hand. She took his hand and stood in the puddle, letting water cascade down her legs and her raincoat. She wanted to scream in anger.

"Stay there, Harris!" Mr Graham transfixed the boy with a finger and watched his expression curdle. "You all right, Pam?"

"I'm wet . . ."

"What happened?"

"I got pushed."

"Harris . . . ! You get to my office. Now."

Harris looked up at Mr Graham in bitter silence.

"Now!"

Harris shrugged off the headmaster and his school and turned away.

"Mr Graham . . ." Pam stepped out of the puddle. "It wasn't him."

Darcy Harris stopped.

"What?"

"He didn't push me into the puddle."

11

Harris looked at her as if she had grown a tail.

"Oh. You sure? Barney, then?" In deep surprise.

"Oh no. Not him."

"Who did, then?"

Pam blinked at Mr Graham. She thought: You tell him and it's worse than asking for homework. You'll be alone on a hill forever. She said: "I—ah— don't know."

And now Barney was looking surprised.

"Really? You didn't see who pushed you?"

"They were wearing yellow raincoats. I'm freezing."

"Of course. Get inside. I'll send someone to help you dry out a bit before your bus arrives." Mr Graham nodded at the door and walked toward the crowded shelter sheds.

Harris jabbed a cocked thumb at Mr Graham's retreating back, then turned to Pam. "Why'd you do that?"

"You didn't do it," Pam said simply and wad- dled towards the school.

Harris let her go a few steps from him, then called: "I need no favours."

2

Darcy turned to face Barney. "Yeah? What are you looking at?"

Barney looked at him. "You're a creep, Darcy."

Darcy took a step back, hunched and beckoned with his open hands. "Make something of it? C'mon, c'mon."

Barney touched his lower stomach. "Yeah, you're great when nobody's looking."

"Well, now's your chance."

Barney moved forward, then stopped and dropped his hands. "I've got better things to do." He walked into the rain.

"Sure you have! Cows are safer," Darcy shouted and swung away, into the distant cold eyes of Mr Graham. He snorted and turned his back on both of them.

Why are you hanging around here, anyway? The rest of the day is all yours. Do something with it.

He leant against the wind and slopped steadily across the bitumen until the blare of a heavy horn stopped him, almost caused him to stumble. He looked up to see the grille of an old bus, leaking steam into the wet air. The wipers scratched quickly across the windscreen, as if the bus was barely controlling its temper. The horn blared again. So Darcy stood where he was.

The door wheezed and slammed open. "Get the hell outa here, kid!" the driver shouted.

Darcy drifted to one side and kicked the front tyre of the bus before he moved on.

Now what was he going to do? He could go down to the bridges, the long Richmond bridge and the low Yarramundi, and watch the river come over the top. But that wouldn't happen for hours yet. Or go home. Oh yes, with Ma watching TV—all the time—and Pop slouching round the place looking for a fight. Great. Just go for a cruise through the town, see what you can do . . .

"Hey, Darce?" A small long-faced boy, Uli Schmander, broke from a group of yellow-coated kids at the corner. "Did she put us in?"

"Browning? She didn't even know who you were."

Uli turned and shouted at the others. "Hey, we're okay!"

The gang broke from the corner and gathered round Darcy, grinning, pushing each other, blowing steam into Darcy's face. Darcy knew them all far too long, knew that Uli's gang would be his gang if he so much as snapped his fingers. Cockroaches trying to walk like wolves. Who needs them?

Uli slapped Darcy on the arm and grinned. "Hey, how was she, Goldilocks? 'Please can we have more work, Miss Rader, 'cause I'm so sweet.' She won't do that again. Lightning raiders!"

"Big deal gangsters."

The grin died on Uli's face.

"Graham was gunna get *me* for that."

"Oh. Sorry, Darce." Uli looked obliquely at Darcy. "You didn't have to tell him who . . ."

Darcy stared him into silence, then pushed through the gang. He strode quickly down the road, away from them.

Lardheads. And they think they're like you. Yeah. When I grow a tail.

Darcy saw a red Ford truck ploughing toward him, throwing an arc of water across the footpath. He ran at the truck, swung his boot into the flooded gutter and hurled a muddy sheet across the windscreen. He heard the brakes squeal as the truck passed him.

And Browning, she had to do her Wonder Woman bit. Truth, Justice and the American Way. If Uli hadn't got her I would've. Might've. Probably. So long as she feels good about it.

Darcy stopped under the awning of George's Café and saw his reflection in the window. A big, square boy with wide, flat eyes, blotches on his face and dark hair dripping onto his forehead. Big and mean, and he was in a good mood.

But Browning didn't make Graham feel good. What a pity, Mister G. You didn't score this time. Next time, hey? But it's a long war and I got to win, baby. Got to. I got nothing to lose.

Darcy clicked his teeth at the image in the window, then looked through the image to see some third graders wrestling with the video games.

End of war. Maybe this flood will take the school, Graham, Pop, the lot of them . . .

He stepped inside and four of the boys immediately muttered and moved aside. But the boy who was pushing his animated character up a mountain of rolling boulders would not budge.

"Whatcha doing?" Darcy, big Darcy, said behind the boy's neck.

"Playing." The boy's hands and fingers were dancing.

"Yer doing all right."

"Yeah. 'Cept people keep bothering me."

Darcy frowned. "Yeah?" He leaned back and nudged the back of the boy's legs with his knees.

The animated character tumbled down the boulders, but recovered. "Leave me alone," said the boy, without taking his eyes from the screen.

"Darcy?" The assistant called from behind the counter.

Darcy nudged the boy again.

"You want to buy something here, Harris?" Louder this time. "Or d'you want to leave?"

Darcy gave the assistant two seconds of the evil eye, bumped the boy out of the way with his hip and strode out. He had the satisfaction of hearing the boy's cry as a rumbling crash finished the game.

The road and the footpath were becoming a lake, with cars becoming slowly moving islands. People were crossing the lake on their toes, battling the wind, the rain and the driven spray. Darcy shrugged and splashed across the water, feeling his shoes filling, his socks squelching and getting heavier.

He looked back at the one piece of art he could understand. On the two-storey side wall of a shop someone had painted a large maze, trapping an old

16

man, a woman, a farmer and others. The one person to find a way out of the maze was a young man, like him, but he was blocked by a huge rejecting hand from the massive consortium of industry, technology and business. In one corner of the painting was the legend: "No job without training, no training without a job." And this was waiting for him, maybe two years away.

He'd been held back a year already. He was older, bigger, tougher than anyone in the school and some of the kids giggled and called him The Prisoner of Primary behind his back. He would probably be held back next year, but that was going to be Graham's worry, not his.

Behind him he heard a heavy car accelerate, hit the lake, splutter and die. He turned to see a middle-aged woman turning the key vainly on a late model Falcon and an old man shaking the spray from his trousers. A farmer with an old cowboy hat and a face scored by the sun purred to the gutter on a mud-coated trail bike.

"Ah, well . . ." The cowboy nodded at the woman in the lake, shrugged and grinned at Darcy.

Darcy did not move.

The grin faded. "What's the matter, kid? Can't you help?"

"Not my car."

The cowboy looked at Darcy as if at something dying messily on the tip of his boot. He swung from the bike and waded to the car.

Darcy watched him go and held the shout coiled on his tongue.

Little judges, they're Batman and Robin. So everybody has to follow them. Shoulda hit him.

Darcy looked at the trail bike. He preferred the line of a trail bike to the heavier, fatter road machine. A trail bike was all skeleton and muscle, a flying dinosaur, an eye and a tooth. This one was not all that old, now that the rain was washing the mud from the chrome. A Kawasaki KX80 with a foxtail attached to a high aerial behind the seat, the exhaust still hot enough to turn falling rain into steam. Another plaything for the farm kids.

He thought about Barney Stevens. Probably home on his farm now, warm, dry, watching TV. Rich kid, knows where he's going to be ten years away because his pa's going to fix it all for him. Everyone gets a push-start.

Except you. Okay, you don't need anything from anyone.

The key was still in the bike.

You're on your own.

Darcy looked up sharply. The cowboy was pushing the Falcon, leaning hard, his knees dipping into the water. The pavement spilled six men and shouting boys around the Falcon and the Falcon began to move.

The key was still in the bike and the engine was still on. You wouldn't believe it.

3

Barney stopped under the Hanging Tree and looked out toward the river, now only a dim dark line of trees and maybe the cliff-line of the other side. The air was heavy with scudding, swirling water and battering wind and he could not toss aside the feeling that he was peering down through a stormy sea at a drowned valley.

He tried to remember how the valley had been— a week ago, a few days ago, a few *hours* ago. On a normal sunny August day he would stand under the old willow tree and see the exact line between Sydney and the country. He would see the houses of Richmond crowded together on the low hills and the brown grass lapping at the fences and sweeping across the Lowlands to a slowly wandering river. On the Lowlands there were very few houses, just a few standing on stilts and some rickety old shacks on knolls waiting for the river to rise. The rest was orchards, dairy cattle and horses. Barney had often sat under the Hanging Tree and watched foals frolicking by the river, three kilometres away.

Now he could see only the grey of the grass and the black humps of cows pushing into each other for shelter. There had been floods before, many floods, dull floods, messy floods, even picnic floods—but none of them would match the one that was coming.

A howling gust of wind bent the willow and tore Barney from its trunk. Barney staggered against the wind for a few paces, his fingers touching the ground, then he realized that if he stopped struggling the gust would blow him home. He turned, felt the wind pressing hard against his back, and began to totter down the hill. He grinned and watched his feet shuffle a long way ahead of his body. His raincoat flattened against his body and he became a walking, running sail.

As he passed he shouted at Kelly, the heavy white horse in the upper paddock, and raised his arm to wave. A gust funnelled under his arm and sent him sprawling under Kelly's nose. Kelly cocked his big head and rippled his lips.

"Oh, shutup." Barney pulled himself to his feet and shook mud from his raincoat.

Kelly nudged his shoulder and waited. Barney surrendered and stroked his nose. He wondered what it would be like to ride Kelly at full gallop in this wind.

Better, ride Kelly at a canter, standing erect on the hindquarters and leaning into the wind. Feel like Superman.

Since someone had furtively left the white horse in the upper paddock one night Barney had named him and gradually assumed the horse was his. He had learnt to ride Kelly over a long summer on the

Lowlands, then rode him standing, standing on one leg and briefly on his head. He had not yet been caught and Kelly did not mind at all, but he had brought home a few bruises.

Barney blew up Kelly's nose and whooped down the hill as the horse snorted. Barney tore past the verandah of his house, clutched the corner post and pulled himself out of the wind.

"You're home," said his father. He was pulling on his yellow boots with effort on the verandah. Reg Stevens wasn't a great talker.

"The bridges are going to go."

Dad slapped his boot. "Yeah. Change. Meet us at the bottom paddock." He pulled himself to his feet and stamped around on the boards.

"The heifers?"

"With your calf, still." He plodded into the storm.

Barney smiled and entered the house.

"Take your feet off!" Mum shouted at him without turning her head.

Barney prised his sodden shoes from his feet, peeled the socks off and threw them behind him. He sniffed the warm floury aroma of oven-fresh scones. "Hi, Mum. I'm terrible hungry," he said hopefully.

"Hi yourself. You'll get fed when those heifers are safe. Mick's down there, already, getting the cows up." She thumbed him through the kitchen.

Barney sighed loudly in a final and hopeless effort, and hurried into his bedroom. His work clothes were already on his bed.

They didn't close the school to get the kids across the bridges, he thought. Oh no, they closed the

21

school because Dad told them to. So he'd get you out there in the mud.

He stripped. He put on his rough cotton shirt, the dungarees, the long, thick socks, the yellow waterproof trousers, the raincoat before he saw the lizard, staring at him from the rim of his swimming trophy, tongue pushed from its mouth. Barney started, then moved carefully toward the trophy.

"That's all right, fellah, won't hurt you . . ." He plucked the lizard from the trophy, felt the plastic and flicked it onto his bed. "Thanks, Mike," he muttered. He carried his hat and his boots back to the kitchen.

"It's a terrible day, Barney," Mum said.

"Oh, I dunno." Barney stopped with his hand on the doorknob.

"Of course, it's not so terrible to you, I know. Anything to dodge school Get away."

Barney stepped outside and watched a tree flogging the air as he worked the boots on. He supposed that he had become one of the Stevens family myths. Like Dad not knowing anything about anything but cows. Fine until you asked him about quasars, Nicaragua, Beethoven or anything. Like Mick absolutely hating cows, the dairy and doing the books. Except you heard him argue with Dad for weeks about introducing new Friesian stock to the herd. Like Mum being sweet and delicate and easy to push around. Except Mick called her Atilla out of earshot. So everyone round the farm knew the only thing Barney liked about school was the rugby team. Except he really liked the books, the problems that challenged him to think, even liked most of the teachers. But say that out loud on the

Stevens corner of the world and you'd get laughed all the way to the dairy. He stood up and stamped a little.

Mum pushed the door open with a glass of milk and a buttered scone. "Quickly now, they're waiting for you."

"Thanks, Mum." And the milk was gone.

"You be careful now. Cows are not the be-all. You tell your father that."

"Oh no. Never." With a mouth full.

A smile played around Mum's face for a moment. "We're getting winds of 75 kilometres an hour. Never seen it like this. Be careful, and I'm serious."

"Sure. 'Bye." He rammed the hat on his head.

Barney walked down the hill toward the Lowlands by the silver ribbon of the macadam road, watching water build little waves around his boots every time he took a step. He had never seen so much water in the air and on the ground before a flood.

A confused mob of cows and horses blocked the road, an old man with an old hat and a pipe standing in the middle of them like a policeman on traffic duty. Barney waited and watched the Stevens cows ignore Clement Lloyd and plod through an open gate. By now they knew exactly where to go. Clement's horses also were used to the old flood routine and separated from the cows to continue walking up the hill. They would stay in the Stevens top paddock until the flood receded then return to their riverside paddock and live on expensive baled hay until the grass grew back.

The horses, bowed and shiny in the wet, moved

past Barney with their eyes half-closed against the wind. Glenda, a brown four-year-old opened an eye as she neared him, recognized him and swung her head at him.

"Get out, you mule." Barney rubbed Glenda's ear and moved on.

Clement turned with the last horse and raised a hand in greeting. "They're down there, Reg and Mick. Join you after I put this mob away, 'kay?"

"Yeah. See you, Clem."

"Filthy lousy weather, innit?"

Barney walked to the flat with streams roaring in the gutters beside the road. When he reached the Lowlands the streams had risen from the gutters and spread. The road had disappeared and he had the uncomfortable sensation of walking along the centre of a river. He had to look hard for the gutter pipes before he was confident enough to step from the road toward the lower gate. The water was far shallower in the heifer paddock, but the ground opened beneath his feet, sucked at his boots with every step. Ahead Dad was shouting at a motion-less mass of cows while Mick looked on.

"Hi, Mick," he yelled.

The big brother lifted a hand to acknowledge him.

"Where'd you catch the dragon?"

"Dragon?"

"The swimming dragon."

"Ah. Thought it needed a home."

"Have to work out where to put it next . . ."

Mick fingered his lip thoughtfully. "Have to watch it, eh?"

Barney thumbed the heifers. "Won't they

24

move?"

"They will. They just need a push to get them going. Like some people we know."

"Some other people we know aren't doing anything much either."

Mick threw a casual headlock on Barney and bopped him lightly. "Reg is best at yelling. You know that."

"Oh, yeah." Released, Barney rubbed his ears and suddenly smiled.

The calf shuffled backwards out of the press of heifers, looked at him and bleated. A bad-tempered bleat. Today was the calf's last day with the heifers. Barney had first seen her in the early morning four days ago, gleaming, new-born, rickety and with wonder in her eyes. She had been trying to bite the sun. Now, almost as nimble as a foal, she had learnt where the food was, when to get it, and which snappy heifers to avoid. And that Barney was not quite another calf. Barney had named her.

"Here, Cuddles," Barney called.

Cuddles propped, stretched her neck toward Barney and sniffed.

Mick looked at Barney blandly. "Be a few steaks in her, I reckon."

"She's not worried. Are you, Cuddles?"

The herd finally decided to move toward the gate and the calf wobbled to the side of its mother, a mean black cow called Darth Vader.

"That's better," said Dad and squelched after Darth Vader.

"Clem's quick," said Mick and walked at the side of the herd.

Barney looked at the road and saw the yellow-coated man in the hat standing outside the open gate. He waved.

Clem waved back, then took a wide step back to allow the herd to pass.

And disappeared.

4

Pam was wringing out her dress in the staff kitchen when the Marjorie girl barged in, holding a battered recorder like a club as she clumsily banged her bag against a wall. She might have been leading a Viking raid, or something.

"Hi, you in trouble?" she said cheerfully.

Pam was cold, wet, angry and embarrassed. Fortunately a wave of heavy rain hit the roof and drowned her reply.

Marjorie shouted as the rolling crash died a little. "Graham caught me by the ear. Said all the teachers—he means women teachers—were too busy to help. I wasn't waiting for a bus, so could I help. So can I help?"

Pam looked up darkly. Oh, he'd done it now. Probably did it on purpose. Deliberately ignored all her friends and picked the school's wet mop. Now Marjorie would be telling everyone how she'd saved her 'dear friend, Pam' for at least a week. That would mean the A-Team would avoid *her* like the plague for at least a fortnight now. She would have to explain.

"No," Pam said.

The brightness faded from Marjorie's face. "Okay," she said and stepped out of the door.

"Ah, wait." What did it matter? Marge would talk about her running around in her knickers anyway.

Marjorie stopped. "They got you, didn't they?"

Pam flared her dress angrily, flinging muddy water across the carpet and up the wall. "See what they did? Look at the tear!"

"That was Uli and the others, wasn't it?"

Pam studied Marjorie's face. "You're on their side, aren't you? Calling me Goldilocks."

"No."

"Think I'm Teacher's Pet."

"Uli's a slug."

The two girls looked at each other in silence. Then Pam nodded. "I'm going to get it, for sure."

"Why? Graham feels sorry for you. Nobody's blaming you."

"At school, maybe. It's different at home."

"Ah, come on . . ."

Pam winced up a poor smile.

"Yeah. My mum carries on a bit when I bring some damage home. I forgot. But we ought to do something about drying you off."

"They probably blame me for the rain."

"Hey, I know where there's a sports tunic. Get it on, shove the dress into your bag and we're away!" Marjorie waggled a finger and whipped back through the door.

Sports tunic? Whose? Hers? Anyone's? Better the wet dress.

Pam wrinkled her nose and closed the door

behind the bouncing girl.

Marjorie had been no more than a shadow in the fifteen months of Pam's school life in Richmond, and she didn't really want to change that. Marge was a big lollopy girl who played soccer with Barney sometimes, who wore old dresses with a lot of stitches and swam in a ghastly swimsuit that made her look like a bumble bee. She had her brown hair tossed all over her head and still had a smear of big freckles across her nose. She went around like a big wet puppy dog and she was embarrassing.

Pam had learnt about everyone from the A-Team since the team had taken her in a year ago. As a result of the team's appraisal Pam knew that Marge was stupid, had an accent taken from some cattle station, and had a mother so allergic to the sun she only moved about by moonlight. There were other things, but that was enough.

Pam found some dishtowels in a drawer and dried her arms and legs as the first bus lurched off into the grey and the second splashed to a stop in its place. The shelter shed began pouring a bumpy yellow stream into its side as the long streak of Miss Rader shimmered alongside. The third bus, the Yarramundi bus, would be along in about half an hour to make sure it caught the latecomers. She would be a little drier when it came, but not much.

Thing was, Marge was not interesting enough to be taken apart. Jan could do her Crocodile Dundee speech and her funny walk, but after that what was there? Now Darcy Harris, that was Quasimodo, the Wolf Man and Frankenstein all rolled into one. You could do Darcy for all of an hour . . .

Pam finished with the towels and felt surprisingly cold. She looked around the kitchen, the hooked teachers' mugs—one leering at her—the stacked plates, the cupboard, the big tin of coffee, the radiator. She stopped. The heater was high on the wall, so high it had string for a switch. Just possibly . . .

She pulled the string and watched the long bar of glass and wire begin to glow. She listened for the heavy tread of a teacher, then draped her dress over the bristles of the broom and lifted it to the heater.

"That's a great idea." Marge had come back. She still moved about like a herd of elephants.

The dress was starting to steam, but the broom and its load were becoming heavy. Pam looked over her shoulder at the purple bundle Marge was carrying away from her body, as if it was rubbish she was about to throw away. "That it?"

"It's not the best," Marge conceded, holding it in both hands and allowing it to unroll. "But it's all I could find."

"Wait a bit." Pam looked around, then placed the handle of the broom in the sink and jammed it to one side with the coffee tin and the leering mug. The dress was held a handspan from the heater.

The purple tunic belonged to someone far larger than Pam. It had a deep orange stain on the front and trailed a few long threads from its frayed hemline. It was covered with tufts of lint, almost as if someone was trying to grow a cotton crop on the purple.

"Well, it's dry."

Pam sniffed it without touching. "It pongs. Whose is it?"

"Dunno. Saw it jammed behind the lockers. Maybe a teacher's." Marge tilted her head to look at it.

"Think I'll wait for my dress to dry."

Marge shrugged and placed it on the kitchen bench. "Why did they do it, anyway?"

"I asked about the homework."

"Oh, yes."

Pam waited for the sneer.

"But you didn't mean homework to do," Marge was frowning. "You meant homework we've done. The projects. It was all a mistake."

Pam looked at Marge in astonishment. As if an elephant was humming a tune. "Yes. Now everyone hates me."

"I don't."

"Oh?"

"Finished that river thing, too. Uli wouldn't have done any work at all. You tell Graham?"

"How?"

"I don't know. But I will." Pam adjusted her dress on the broom so a new wet patch faced the heater.

Marge leaned back and looked at Pam slyly. "You could get him now."

"He's not here."

"But his desk is. And the teachers are out there."

Pam thought a moment. "I don't want to steal things . . ."

"We don't have to. Let's have a look."

Pam reached for the sports tunic, then changed her mind and slipped into her raincoat. She followed Marge into the corridor, checked that it *was* empty and ran lightly to the classroom. It was alarmingly large and hollow. Marge slid to Uli's desk, banged it open and clapped her hands.

"Shut up!" Pam hissed.

Marge ran her fingers over the dog-eared books, the broken pencil-case, the mysterious tassel of fur. "Maybe we can put something in there. Like —chalk?"

"Chalk?"

"Go and get some blackboard dusters, bang them all over his books and everything."

Pam raised her finger and waved it about. "Better, better." She ran back to the kitchen, snatched her schoolbag from the bench and galloped up to Marge. She opened her bag hurriedly and buried her arm in it up to the elbow for a few moments.

"What is that?" Marge said.

"Perfume. Like a sniff?"

Marge sniffed. "What are you doing with that? Does your mum know?"

"Sure. I can wear it out of school. Maybe even lipstick."

Marge was impressed.

"So . . ." Pam pointed the nozzle into the desk and pressed the button. Hyacinths and musk wafted across the corridor.

"Oh, that's terrible, really terrible." Marge said, and giggled. "Rambo Schmander with all his books smelling like—that!"

Pam closed the desk thoughtfully. "Maybe get the others too. Never get a better chance."

Marge tapped at the scarred desk behind her own. "And get Harris. Gives me bruises all over my back."

Pam grinned, then frowned. Something was

happening, had been happening for several minutes, and she did not know whether she wanted it to happen at all. The elephant was beginning to fly. "Ah no. He'd know."

"Yes, I suppose. But one day . . ." Marge looked up and sniffed.

Pam caught a slight bitter wisp through the heavy paddocks of flowers and ran from the classroom. She skidded through the doorway of the staff kitchen and saw two things at the same time.

Out the window her bus, the Yarramundi bus, was being loaded at least twenty minutes ahead of schedule.

And her dress was on fire.

5

Darcy looked back at the farmer in the cowboy hat, surrounded now by kids and wet adults. The woman in the car looked uncomfortable, as if she was worried that her neighbours would get to know about her embarrassment. The cowboy was smiling, winking at her as he pushed, as if she was his mother.

Not like the look he threw at you over the handlebars, the old 'you're nothing, kid, we don't need you, kid'. They all had it. Graham, Pops, Sergeant Henderson, even snotty kids like Stevens had it, they learn from each other. That cowboy, he won't even remember you. There's nothing worth remembering.

Darcy dropped his eyes to the softly growling trail bike, the glistening silver-spoked front wheel turning slowly in the air, the steam coiling from the length of the exhaust, the spare body trembling slightly on the stand. It was speaking to him.

You can ride this, Darcy thought, and the thought frightened him. He shook it away and wiped his hands on his black raincoat.

The thought slithered back. You've ridden Pop's old BSA, heavy and fat, like riding an elephant— until Pop rode it off a cliff chasing rabbits. Oh, sure, it was a bit of trouble, and you didn't ever let it fall because it took hours to get it back up, but you could ride it. This Kawasaki lightweight, hell, you could take it away with one arm and one leg.

Couldn't you?

The cowboy stepped back from the car and began to turn toward Darcy.

Darcy heard the air sighing into his lungs. His mouth was open and suddenly he was in the air, his grey raincoat rasping. For a moment he felt that he was still standing on the pavement watching some other boy rush past him. But his hands slipped down on the handlebars, fingers curling round the thick grips and that other boy was him! His body hit the saddle with an impact that forced air from his lungs and heaved the bike off its stand. The bike wobbled in his hands, leaned hard on his left hand, and someone was shouting behind him. He could hear quick splashes, like running on water.

The bike roared, reared from the water and he was falling.

The cowboy was going to catch him, throw him into the lake and everyone would laugh. Laugh for months.

He stabbed down with a foot, the bike slewed, other foot, lost the seat, spray, rain, waves every-where. The bike was ploughing toward George's Café . . . He hurled his body to the right, the bike twisted and the open road swung before him. The front wheel dipped into the water and the bike scudded down the road, with Darcy searching for a seat.

The cowboy bellowed from the centre of the road, but it was from a distance.

Darcy found the pedals, shifted his weight and felt the bike steady and moving into his control. He took a corner, left the road, bounced down a nature strip and regained the road again. He decelerated a touch, took two more corners and looked back. There was nobody chasing him any more.

"Yehay!" he shouted.

What you do that for?

Shutup.

He accelerated to the bike's limit on a straight stretch of road, allowing the rain to blind him, the wind to force itself down his throat. But ahead there were no houses to shelter the road and the trees were being tossed about like tussocks of grass. He sensed the danger soon enough to lower his body and bring his speed down, but not enough to avoid it. A gust slammed him in the face like a padded truck. The bike was stopped in five metres, turned and pushed back down the road. He fought to stay on his wheels for a few seconds, then ran into an embankment backwards. But somehow he held the bike upright and was able to ride on when the gust eased.

Hey, why Sergeant Henderson? Why did you think of the fat cop before you took off?

Darcy looked over his shoulder.

He doesn't know you exist. When he comes round he looks through you like you're a sheet of glass. He's Pop's trouble, not yours.

Until now.

Having a bit of the collywobbles, are we? The

cowboy, he'll never remember what you look like, right? Forget it.

You just about rode into George's Café. There were others.

No one you knew. Who's going to point the finger?

Come on. Just about everybody. The whole world. Just love the chance.

Big deal.

Henderson may be on your tail.

He'll have to catch me!

Darcy rolled the accelerator back and felt the beat of the engine in his bones. Remembering the good time before the BSA went over the cliff, the times when Pops couldn't ride, couldn't give a lizard, and he was sent out on the bike to pick up things. You could stay away from the house for hours and hours . . . No, no, that wasn't a good time, the only good time was *after* the BSA went over the cliff, when Pops had a broken leg and couldn't do anything but shout and sulk. That was almost okay.

Darcy swept to a low crest and saw that Rickaby's Creek had left its bed. It was now swirling around the posts of its bridges and foaming across the road before him. He started to slow down, then shook his head and lifted his feet from the pedals.

What's the matter Pop, can't you swing now? Even Ma played up, treated him like a caged gorilla. Great if he broke the other leg . . .

Darcy hit the water. Rickaby's Bridge normally passed over a large gully with a drowsy creek meandering along the bottom but now there was no gully, no creek. This was a river charging toward the sea with only a flat stretch of road in the way. The bike immediately lost half its wheels in the rushing water, the exhaust began to bubble and Darcy realized that the creek was travelling far faster than he was. The bridge was almost past, but he was being pushed sideways, being forced to lean against the rush.

Wake up, wake up . . .

The back wheel started to skid and the engine coughed and died. Darcy put a foot down, had it swept under the bike and fell into the flood. He tried to shout, but his mouth filled with water as he and the bike seemed to spin around each other. He could feel the ground sliding past him but too fast to push against, far too fast to stand on, and he couldn't seem to find the surface of the water to breathe air. Any moment now, the gully would open beneath him.

He was clawing blindly at the water when he was thrown at a muddy bank. He shoved his hands into the mud, lifted his head and gasped. He scrabbled clear of the flood and stood still for a minute, hands on his knees and whooping.

"Ah, bloody hell . . ."

He closed his eyes, opened them and saw the bike being pushed against a log two metres away. He waded quickly into the current and caught a handlebar before he realized what he was doing. He thought of dropping the bike and getting out of the water fast and for good, but he stayed in the water and dragged and wrestled the bike onto the road.

"Won't go now. That's for sure."

He kicked the starter and some water came out of

the exhaust. He kicked it again and thought of pushing it back into the creek. He kicked it again and thought of the distance he would have to walk now. He kicked it again and the bike started.

"Hey, hey, hey!"

Darcy leapt on the bike and rode it into the wind. The bike coughed and shuddered a few times in the first minutes, then settled down to a satisfying metallic growl.

Don't worry about the cops. Don't worry about Pop. That's tomorrow and maybe you won't even see it. Now you can skid across Graham's front lawn, drive Uli's mice off the road, stampede Mick Stevens' cows. *Now* is everything, the whole smear!

He aimed the bike at a partially collapsed gate and soared into a paddock of mud and water. He took off his grey raincoat while he skirted a great bowl of mud, holding it around his neck by a single button. He drove the bike into the mud, skidding, slewing, shimmying, jumping hillocks, making it dance. He covered his shoes, his legs, his face with a thick layer of rich, heavy mud, filling the air with flying pools of black syrup.

Darcy pulled back on the handlebars to rear the bike, a skeletal silver horse, before the rolling purple clouds and the torn lightning. He stood on the pedals with his mouth wide open, catching the wind and the sleeting rain. Thunder crashed across the sky as the raincoat billowed high from his shoulders turning the boy into a creature immense and terrible.

"Go on. Go on. What can you do?" Darcy yelled at the storm. "I beat you!"

6

"Clem's gone!" Barney shouted.

He ran through the mud to the gate, slithering past Darth Vader and an old cow, stopped and blinking at the flooded hole near the gutter. In the water was Clem's old hat and his corn cob pipe.

In horror, Barney took a step into the gutter, but was thrust back by Mick. Mick squared himself at the end of the gate and shook himself out of his heavy plastic coat. He stabbed a finger at Barney.

"You stand back and watch!" he shouted and swung his arms back for a racing dive.

And the hat rose from the water. And the pipe. And the dripping figure of Clem.

Mick took a stumbling step, skidded and fell backwards.

Clem pulled himself out of the hole against the rush of water in the gutter. He seized clumps of grass, the gate and finally Barney's hand.

"Suppose I'll never hear the end of this," he said.

"Thought you'd gone, Clem," Reg said. He was keeping his face grave, but with effort.

"Tell you, Reg, that was a very long time down

there."

"How deep is it, then?"

"I was sitting down."

"Oh."

"Shows you have to keep eyes in your head."

"Wish you'd decided to come up before I took the coat off." Mick was wriggling back into the coat but it was a lost cause. He was almost as sodden as Clem.

"Well, you'd better get home," Reg said. "Dry up. We can take it from here."

"What about me?" Mick said pitifully.

"Steam it off."

"Very funny."

Barney pointed urgently across the road. "Look at Darth Vader!"

"I'll barbecue that cow!"

"Seeya Clem."

The heifers had dutifully walked past the men and the boy at the gate and turned up the road toward their waiting upper paddock. Except for Darth Vader. On the other side of the road were some of the finest turf paddocks in the State, producing front lawns for houses all over Sydney. There were no fences around these paddocks, as turf has not yet been known to walk.

So Darth Vader had strolled across the road and was leaving a trail of deep hoof marks across the turf in search of the perfect mouthful.

Barney ran-splashed into the turf paddock with Mick behind him. "Vader! C'mon, Darth Vader!"

"Hey, hey, shutup." Mick slowed Barney with a heavy hand on his shoulder. "Panic that cow and she'll gallop all over the paddock. Softly softly, right?"

"Okay, softly." Barney began to walk across the turf as though it contained mines.

Darth Vader turned her head, glared at Barney and moved deeper into the paddock.

Mick stopped and rubbed the side of his nose. "That won't do. That cow is getting too fidgety, and it's all your mate's fault." He opened his hand in a helpless sign to Reg, waiting on the road.

"What mate?"

"Caught him heaving clods of mud at Darth Vader. No wonder she's playing hard to get. Tell you, I clipped him."

"Which mate?"

"The Harris kid. Ah well, we'll have to get past her."

"Darcy Harris?" Barney drifted from Mick's side.

"Yeah, him. Lives in a shack near Yarramundi. If I catch him again I'll have Sergeant Henderson on him. You tell him that."

"Not my mate. Nobody's mate."

Barney sloshed quickly toward a hill far across the turf. Mick walked off at an angle and neither of them glanced at the cow. Darth Vader watched them both with deep suspicion but without moving. She nibbled grass slightly below the water.

Barney stopped when the cow was closer to the road than he was and waited for Mick. Mick turned off the cow's flank and clapped. Darth Vader stopped chewing and looked up at Mick. She snorted and looked away, to an approaching Barney, also slowly clapping. The cow turned from them both and walked sadly back toward the

42

road.

Lovely piece of work, if I say so myself, thought Barney. He looked beyond the defeated Darth Vader for a sign of approval from his father, but Reg had gone on to see the heifers into the top paddock.

Well, what did you expect—a medal? No, this is as it should be. You're expected to do a job, and do it well, and that's that. You're not a kid any more. Not down here.

Barney squelched behind the cow, feeling a slight glow despite the rain and the wind.

The cow finally left the turf but stopped on the road as if she was trying to remember something. But when she saw the heifers climbing the slope she actually hurried to catch them. Mick joined Barney and they walked easily up the road, the job done.

"But that cow's got to go." Mick chopped the air with his hand after Darth Vader.

"Don't think she did much damage, did she?"

"Not this time. The flood's going to do all the damage tonight."

"You reckon it's going to be bad?"

"Look at it now. We don't need the river to put us under this time, just the rain. You won't be paddling about tomorrow."

"You won't be playing footy, either."

"Maybe water polo?"

"Ha ha. How high d'you reckon she'll come?"

"The house fence? She could do that. But no worries, we'll be sitting on top of it. Us and the air force on our islands. Out with the old Monopoly game."

Dad closed the top paddock gate behind Darth

Vader as he looked out across the Lowlands to the river. "Think she's coming."

What had been a brown glimmer, a tickle of the imagination through the trees, was now a distant stain around a knoll.

Fine, the river was getting ready to break its banks. Two days, maybe three of doing nothing at all. Except a little bit of paddling when the river started to recede.

Barney looked up at the yellow fibreglass Canadian canoe upended near the farmhouse, and smiled.

This super flood, it could be an adventure. It could be fun.

"Hey . . ." Dad was passing a slow finger over the herd, frowning. "Where's the calf?"

7

Pam jumped for the burning broom as she yelled.

But everything else was happening slowly. She was in the air, arms outstretched, as flames from her dress licked gently at the ceiling of the teachers' kitchen. Her fingers touched the broom handle and she saw that it had slipped in the sink, pushing the sweeping head and the dress against the heater. She closed her hands on the handle and pulled it from the sink as a piece of flaming material unfolded on her arm. She squealed and stumbled backwards. The dress flopped to the floor and burned against a cupboard.

What do I do? What do I do? She banged her fists together.

Marge pushed past her with the broom in her hands, scooped up the dress with the handle, dumped the dress in the sink and turned the tap on full. Pam was engulfed in a cloud of grey steam, and staggered back, coughing. When she could see again Marge was running water over the blackened bristles and almost smiling.

"Close, wasn't it?" Marge said brightly.

Pam looked at the smear of black on the ceiling, the black flame ghost on the cupboard door, the shortened, curly bristles on the broom, and the singed rag that had been her dress.

"Do you think they'll notice?" she said.

Marge shook the broom out over the sink. "Probably. Unless we get flooded out."

"Do you think . . . Stop it. It's serious."

"Not as serious as it could have been. But we stopped it, didn't we?"

"What do we do now?"

"Clean it up and tell someone. They're not going to shoot—"

"My bus!" Pam caught the movement in the window, started to run, remembered that she was wearing only her vest and knickers under her raincoat, hesitated and stopped.

"Go!"

Pam started again, but it was too late. The bus had swept out of the school gate before she had reached the door of the teachers' common room. "They left me. They didn't even look to see. I'm dead." She flopped into a chair.

"They must've thought you'd been picked up by your parents. Hey, that's an idea. Come over to my place, ring your mum and have her pick you up there."

"I suppose . . ."

"And you can get into one of my dresses. My mum won't mind."

Pam scratched the arm of her chair.

"Your mum can pick you up, can't she?"

"Oh yes, no trouble at all."

"Good, that's it then. Let's get this cleaned up a

46

little."

Marge cleaned the floor of blackened fragments of the dress with dishtowels. Pam's attempt to sweep the floor with the burnt brush had left a pattern of black lines, so Marge took over. Pam worked on the cupboard with a wet dishtowel for a few moments then stopped and watched Marge in silence.

You know, she's not all that stupid.

"Come on, come on," Marge said.

But she is still an elephant.

Pam was able to reduce the size of the black flame but Marge decided that the mark on the ceiling was best left alone. They rinsed the cloths, hung them on their rail to drip themselves dry and ran for the school entrance. They nearly ran down Miss Rader on their way out.

"You're still here, Pamela?" Miss Rader looked alarmed. "I didn't know—"

"It's all right, Miss Rader. Mum's going to pick me up."

"Are you sure?"

"Oh yes. Any tick. Oh, Miss Rader, we made a tiny mess in the kitchen drying my dress, but we cleaned it up, and it's all right now. We have to go."

"Mess?"

"Bye." And they were down the steps and through the gate before they could be called back.

Two blocks later, on the edge of the plateau, Marge stopped and panted. "A tiny mess?" She shook her head.

"You said tell them. I told them."

"Sort of."

"Well . . . They might forget when school starts again."

"Oh, yes." Marge nodded, then peered through the rain at the roofs of two houses a step down from the road. "Look at the river."

Pam frowned and then focused on the grey mist between the roofs, saw the dim paddocks of the Lowlands and something moving, swelling behind a distant line of trees.

"It's flooding?" Pam's mouth felt dry. Her family had moved from the hills of Adelaide last year. She was still getting used to life around a river and this was her first flood.

"Not yet. But downstream it'll be getting damp." Very calm, as if this sort of thing happened all the time.

"The bridge? Has the bridge been covered already?"

"Don't think so. But Yarramundi is always the first to go. We'd better get you to the phone."

Marge stamped quickly down the road to a weatherboard house almost besieged by rushing water. The roof gutters released a dozen waterfalls on paths, windows, crumpled flowers; a stream gushed down a jungled slope and banked against a leaning lemon gum before joining a hissing cataract on the road.

"Jump!" shouted Marge and she did.

Pam took a short run, leapt across the gutter and began to fall backwards. She slapped at the thick trunk of the lemon gum for balance and felt it move. She kept her hand on the wood and looked up, watching the branches scything across the sky.

"All right, Pam?" Marge was shouting from the

shelter of the back door.

Pam took her hand carefully from the tree, as if she was holding it up, and ran to join Marge.

"Mum's not here." Marge moved a large flower-pot to show a key. She unlocked the door and stepped aside for Pam.

Pam hesitated. She had forgotten about Marge's Mum. What had Annabel said? Afraid of the sun, only seen when the moon is out, sounds like Dracula . . .

Marge pushed Pam into the house and took off her own raincoat as she backed into the house.

Well, she wasn't here, was she? Probably lying about in a dusty coffin until night . . .

Pam looked about her as she stood on the worn vinyl tiles and dripped. She thought the kitchen was pretty primitive. Two taps instead of one, round corners on the fridge, a white oven looking like an old washing machine, painted wooden cupboards—one cupboard was propped up by a piece of dowel—and not even a dishwasher.

"Well?"

"Well what?" said Pam.

"You've got to take off your raincoat and your shoes here. Else I get my head blown off."

"Oh." Pam shucked off her coat and took off her shoes one-legged. She followed Marge into the bathroom, washing machine jammed beside the vanity, ironing board leaning against the shower nozzle, bath lined with a herd of plastic ponies.

"Do you have a real pony, too?" Pam picked up a pink pony as she dried her face on a faded towel.

"No. I just like them." Marge was going through a laundry basket full of fresh clothes.

"My dad says I can have a pony next year."

"Hey, that's great."

"Maybe I can give you a ride sometimes."

Marge started to smile brightly then stopped, as if weighing Pam's words. "That'd be nice. Here." She threw a school dress at Pam, a little high, catching her on the nose.

"Dad says this place is tops for horses and everything. He says our place across the river is country. This side of the river is city."

"Not much difference."

Pam shrugged into the dress. A bit too big and a bit too faded, but not too bad on the whole. "Well, that's what my dad says. So he traded in our Commodore for a Range Rover. All gold and green. He is a company executive. What does your dad do?"

"You better phone home." Marge led her into the living room and passed her the phone.

Pam dialled and waited, looking around Marge at the room. Shelves of old books, family photos, worn-out furniture and a cat asleep on a couch.

"Hello . . ." A woman's worried voice.

"Hi, Mum."

"Pam! Thank God! I've been so worried about you, the bus just left and you weren't on it. I was out there in the rain, waiting for you, and you weren't there. I was about to call the police. What happened? Where are you?"

"I'm all right Mum. I'm at Marge's place."

"Who's Marge?"

"Just a friend. A new friend."

"Why are you there, and not here?"

"It is complicated. Can you pick me up?"

"Oh, oh, I don't know . . ."

"It's all right, Mum, the bridges are above the water. Just drive across and pick me up and drive back. I'm not very far from the Yarramundi Bridge."

"It's my car. It won't start. Something's wrong with the starter motor. It's in the garage now."

"Oh."

"I don't know what we can do."

"Taxi?"

Marge was shaking her head. "I don't think we can find a taxi this far out. Not today. Not for the Yarramundi Bridge. Hey, you can stay here."

"What's going on?" Mum sounded agitated.

"No taxi." Pam glanced around the living-room again. She looked at Marge and away. "When will Dad be home?"

"He's coming now. But I don't know when he'll be here. The roads are terrible. I don't know . . ."

"You can stay here," said Marge.

"Perhaps you could stay in your friend's house," said Mum.

Pam said: "Umm . . ."

"Until your father comes home," said Mum. "What is the address?"

Pam half-turned to Marge. "Address?"

Marge gave it to her. Crisply.

Pam leaned over the phone. "Sixty-four-Sixty-Mum . . . Mum!" She looked up. "The phone's dead."

8

Darcy dropped the bike from a long rearing charge through the mud and promenaded it almost sedately around the paddock. He liked the feeling, the sense of controlling his pace and direction, the knowledge that he held all the power in the world under his fingers but was hardly touching it. He was a giant with a feather.

It was like lying in the long grass with a dry seedbox tickling his cheek, with his eye locked on the sights of the .22 and a dozy rabbit nibbling upwind. But that was gone, now.

Like cruising the BSA on a quiet road in the hills with the sun at his back and he could ignore home and pretend there was a wild continent waiting for him at the end of that road. Sometimes some great Alsatian would lope along beside him or a couple of bikies would yell, 'Aariiiight!' as they combed past him. But that was gone, now; gone since Pop just had to drive the BSA off that cliff.

But the feeling had died long before that. It had died every time he had to turn for home. Every time he had to swing down from the freedom machine to the mud. Back to the endless push, push, from home to school, from box to box. And when Pop wrecked the BSA and when he took the .22 there was no way out . . .

Darcy saw the old grey van from the back of the paddock. He had not seen it come through the rain, couldn't hear it over the beat of the bike, but there it was, quietly steaming outside the broken gate. It shouldn't be there. What did it think it was doing, taking in a free show?

"Beat it," he muttered. The cold rain washed the mud in streams down his face.

You're probably in his paddock. Yeah, that's it. Here to shout you off his little piece of mud. Maybe call in the cops. They're all like that. If they've got a house, a milk-bar, a trail bike, any stinking little thing, they have to make out they're better than you. That you're nothing. Just another bludger.

Darcy kicked off in a long spray of mud and water, skidding and spinning his wheels in a wild circuit of the paddock. He stopped with a layer of grass and soil flying about him.

How's that, then?

The driver was alone in the van and he seemed to be talking to a radio.

He's really calling up the cops. Going to have a piece of me for chopping up his lucerne. But the cops aren't coming, not now. Too busy keeping little old ladies dry.

Darcy twisted his wrist and the bike shuddered.

But maybe talking about stolen trail-bikes. Maybe for that they'd come.

Darcy looked at the distant driver with his feet

flat on the ground and the bike quietening in his hands. The driver was leaning back and was watching him. Darcy looked around him, at the large paddock, the great pools, the mud, the wild patterns the bike had left, the long wire fences. He was trapped, locked in like a bull in an arena, waiting for the toreador. The only way out of the paddock was the collapsing gate and that van was sitting there. In the way.

Darcy punched the end of a handlebar and shook his head.

It was always like this. Pop was right about that, the only time he ever was right. They're always out there, taking things from you—homes, jobs, places to go—and building barriers, fencing you in.

But he wasn't going to just sit here and wait.

Darcy rode the bike in a broad arc across the paddock, looking at the broken gate and the man in the van. There was a tiny bit of space between the post and the edge of the van's bonnet. Just. He tightened the arc of the bike into a loop and moved toward the gate.

The door of the van opened reluctantly. The bike roared and slewed, kicking a plume of black mud from the back wheel. The driver stood up in the rain, shielded an eye and shouted something. Darcy bent over the handlebars, forgot about the man and concentrated on the broken gate sliding toward him. To come into the paddock he had launched himself from its slope, using it as a ramp. Now he must dodge its high edge, jump the bike on the gate in the gap between the gate and the fence post. He must stay on the slope of the gate and run across it to avoid the van. And it seemed to be just about impossible.

"Hey, kid!" the man yelled.

Darcy wobbled in fright, but did not move his eyes. There was a bent pole from the gate rammed into the mud and there was a ditch on the other side.

"Kid!"

And Darcy jumped, the bike jumped, the back wheel clipped the toppled gate and the bike flew. Darcy glimpsed the driver, an angry eye, a flash of teeth, a clutching hand. The ditch fled past him and the bonnet seemed far too close. But he was down on the road and away. He took his hands from the handlebars and clenched them over his head in triumph.

But when Darcy looked back over his shoulder the driver had climbed back into his van. The van lurched from the side of the road, kicking mud in its wake, and clanged after Darcy.

"Come on, Lardhead, you're beaten," Darcy muttered. But he was suddenly nervous.

He rolled the accelerator back, scudding down the road with black water streaming from his shoulders and the flapping raincoat. He turned into an open road and the bike began to fly under him. The rain seemed to stop falling and flew straight at his face. He wanted to open his mouth and yell.

The van cornered clumsily behind him, rocking deeply as it straightened. The horn blared as the engine roared.

"Leave me alone, will ya!" Darcy yelled.

But the van was gaining. He could look back and watch it grow on the road, from a hump, a rolling egg to an animal with flat eyes and a sneer.

Of course it's catching you, mug. Only got a bigger engine, more power, higher speed limit. Stay on a straight road and you're giving him the whole box. Probably a cop coming down the road ahead now, closing the trap.

He had to get off the road, turn off before it was too late.

The van blared again, far closer now.

But there was nowhere to go. He had driven up the same road he had come down and way up ahead there was Rickaby's Bridge with its crazy brown river and he could hear it now.

But he had crossed the river before. Why couldn't he cross it again? For sure the van wouldn't follow him there.

Darcy saw that the black macadam had become a fast moving tide of brown far beyond the posts of the bridge. The posts were now stumps in the water and something was slowly cracking.

Can't do it now. Couldn't do it then. That was luck. Now it's got a hell of a lot worse. You go in and he will stop on the safe road and watch you get washed away.

Darcy braked and the wheels began to skid and the van blared from Darcy's rear wheel. Darcy squeezed the brakes, the wheels locked and the rear wheel was drifting across the road.

And the bike was facing the van five metres away. The van braked, began to skid and swung away. Darcy saw the open road beyond the van and leapt forward, feeling his right pedal scraping along the side of the van before he broke free. The van stopped, the driver unwound his window and looked down at the damage Darcy had done and

Darcy could still hear the shout over the wind. He lowered his head to the handlebars and aimed at the corner almost a kilometre away.

How's that, Lardhead! You'll never catch us, we're too bloody tough . . .

He could hear the revving and the angry squeal of the van being backed, turning in the narrow road, but he did not look. He could not afford to.

Darcy remembered the day that two of Uli's gang wore paper clips like earrings just to show how tough they were. He had laughed that day and he was laughing now. He had known how tough he was from his third birthday, and had needed no gimmicks since then.

He could hear the roar of the van increase as the driver clanked through the gears, but the corner was sliding up to him.

That was when Pop was in Vietnam, and maybe he was really tough then. That was the time you went into a tree after a ball and fell and saw the broken bone of your arm sticking through the skin, and walked half a mile home to get it fixed. No crying. It does no good to cry when nobody will hear.

Darcy braked and skidded round the corner, aiming for Richmond and the river. The van scudded round three seconds later.

So you've got one more on your back. What's new? Pop, Graham, Barney Stevens' big brother, they get you, and sooner or later you get them back. They never win and this one will never touch you. Relax.

Darcy jerked into a street lined with new brick houses instead of trees and paddocks. He began to weave through streets and lanes like a pencil on a map but the van roared behind him. He skidded round one corner, jabbing frantically at the road to keep the bike under him and when he managed to sway away he was feeling very cold and he had started to pant.

He's going to kill someone, driving like that. He's mad, that's what it is. He's mad . . .

He hit a sheet of water spread right across the road from gate to gate and was thrown forward as the bike seemed to brake. He wound the accelerator back, heard the exhaust bubbling as the front axle disappeared, but he kept on cruising. The van charged up behind him, howling, hissing round the bonnet—

"Bloody hell!"

—and hit the water. The van dropped into its bow wave, creating a rising curtain of steam and a wake, spreading across the street. For a moment the van had become a launch, then the engine died. The van rolled out of the water and stopped.

Darcy drove to the next corner, revved his engine and stopped. He turned in the saddle and thrust his thumb at the sky.

The van steamed, whined several times and coughed.

"Why doncha get out and run, eh?" Darcy yelled.

The van coughed again, spluttered and roared.

"Stoopid . . ." Darcy shook his head and fled round the corner.

The chase seemed to go on forever now. Darcy unbuttoned his raincoat in a bid to blind the van, but the wind whipped it into a tree; the van aimed at Darcy's back wheel and hit a rubbish bin; Darcy was nearly run down by a green Volkswagen and the van spun past it in a wild circle. Darcy rode across the main street of Richmond, recognising it only by the flare of the lights of the shops, swooped down to the Flatlands and climbed back again. After a while he did not know where he was, only that he was cold, wet, half blinded and so tired that his arms were trembling on the handlebars.

He turned into the lane, more to escape the rain and the wind than to escape the van. There were tall buildings on either side, killing the wind, and the sky dripped instead of hurling down an ocean. But Darcy was beginning to believe that the van would be chasing him to the end of his life.

He saw the fence across the lane only half a second before he hit it. He catapulted from the bike, hit the wooden fence with his shoulder and fell back onto the still-spinning rear wheel of the bike. He grunted in pain and rolled to a knee.

The van slid into the lane, spreading its hissing bulk from wall to wall, pinning him with the glare of its lights. It stopped with a sigh and the door opened.

The driver stepped out and put his cowboy hat on his head.

9

Barney followed Dad's finger for a moment then snapped his eyes to the empty road. "Cuddles?" he breathed, and shouted: "Cuddles!"

"All right," Dad said tiredly. "It's not here. Thought you had it."

"Guess we thought it was up here," Mick said.

"You had Darth Vader. The cow. Calves stay with their cows, most times."

"Cow of a cow. You can't blame Cuddles for striking out on its own."

"I can blame Barney. It's your calf, Barney. You named the damned thing. Why couldn't you keep your eye on it?"

"Hey, Reg . . ." Mick opened his hands in protest.

"I'll find it, all right?" Barney pulled some flat bailers' twine from the gate.

Dad's anger petered out. "We'd better do something about it. You and Mick see what you can find."

Mick nodded.

"Watch it, right?"

Barney walked on in silence for a minute or so, trying to pick out the shape of the calf in the grey, rain-swept paddocks or beneath the grey trees.

"Ease off, Young Tiger." Mick, calling from behind.

Barney caught himself almost running down the slope, and slowed and shrugged. "Dad's a bit mad, isn't he?"

"Has to be. Part of the job."

"Suppose so." Barney tried something between a smile and a wince.

"And he should've seen that Darth Vader was alone. We can't catch all the runaway stock in Australia at the same time."

"No."

That is the good thing about Mick. A pain most of the time, goes on and on about his football, his old car—his 'reconstituted Rolls', and there's Julie, and Trish, and Anne. Talks all the time. Except when he's wrecking a model you've been working on for a month, or shoving hay down the back of your neck, or sticking plastic lizards about your room. But when you need a little support he's there. Like a dog with bad breath.

Mick picked a length of the bailers' twine from Barney's shoulder. "We'll find the little pest."

"Wonder where she's gone."

"Well, Barn, if I was a calf, a stupid little calf, I would go downhill because it is easier to walk down than up."

"Toward the river?"

"This one's a very stupid little animal." Mick leaned back into the wind and strolled along the flattening road.

"Can't be far away."

They walked in step beside flattened grass, scarecrows in a rippling sea. They reached the closed gate of the heifer paddock and looked for Cuddles there and in the turf paddocks. There was no sign of the calf.

"This wind . . ." Mick stopped a moment and leaned back to touch the ground. "They say it's getting up to 70 kilometres an hour. No school buildings blown down?"

"Nothing much. We were sent home because the bridges are going to go."

"For sure. Sydney's copped 150 millimetres just today. Now you know how Noah felt."

"Wonder when it's going to stop."

"That's easy. Thirty-nine days."

"Very funny. It could be bad. Couldn't it?"

"Could be? It *is* bad. They've stopped the ferries in Sydney Harbour; the waves are too big. Toongabbie is becoming an island and out Lithgow way someone got drowned trying to rescue someone in a creek. What we don't know is just how bad it's going to get."

Barney stopped at a T-junction and looked about him. "I still can't see her."

"We've had it before. We'll get it again. But we'll remember this one."

"Yeah, but she's gone."

"Oh yeah." Mick stood in the centre of the small junction and tilted his head, as if he was listening for something over the smothered wail of the wind. "Okay, we split. I go right—it's nearer the river—you go left. You give it only twenty minutes. If you haven't got the animal by then, I've got it and I'm dragging it home by the tail. If neither of us has it, it is in the river and that's it. Okay?"

"Okay." Barney walked away.

"And Barn?" Mick was looking after him, his face dripping and suddenly anxious. "You be careful, okay? The river's on its way. Don't get caught."

"Don't worry."

"Well, watch it."

Barney hunched against the sleet and plodded along the road. He did not look back. Everything was grey now, grey, turbulent and frightened. To his right a line of trees marked a raised bank of the river and he could almost hear it hissing past their roots. A ramshackle timber house beside a rusty tower had already been abandoned and the flat paddocks were turning into a lake. A man and a dog were driving several horses with two foals toward the uplands, their coats gleaming in the wet. A black foal turned from the horses and was confronted by the dog. The foal stumbled, the dog barked, the foal propped on its matchstick legs, and a horse, a mare, trotted over to swing its long neck across the foal, pushing it gently on its way.

Why can't cows learn to do that? Barney thought.

The wind punched him in the side and he stepped sideways to recover his balance. He thrust his hands deep in his pockets and walked up a mound for a better view, gaining some little comfort from the sounds of his rubber boots squeaking on the gravel and his warm breath drumming the edge of his hood. He stopped at the top and turned back.

He could see the farm in the distance. There was the house high on the hill and Mum was probably standing in the rain, worrying and looking for Mick and him. She would have taken a piece of Dad's ear for letting them go. She would stay there until she saw them on their way back. He could see the flash of yellow of his canoe and the clump of trees 200 metres down the slope. Last flood those trees looked like bushes and he could paddle out to them. This time? This time they might completely disappear. Further down there was the Mitigation Channel, a ditch with locks to regulate the flow of water into and out of a small lake. He had spent many hours there in the past, fishing for carp and just thinking. But now it had stopped being a channel and become part of a swelling swamp.

He knew what was going to happen tonight and the knowledge dried his mouth. Rain water was flowing from the creeks, Rickabys, South, and the run-off trenches of the RAAF base into the Lowlands and the Hawkesbury. The waters from Grose Vale and the Blue Mountains were tumbling into the Hawkesbury through the raging Grose River. The Hawkesbury was ready to burst its banks in the flat land downstream from Richmond, cut across the curve near Windsor and flood backwards across the Richmond Lowlands. Meanwhile the Warragamba Dam in the hills was full and the spillway was releasing megalitres of water. The Yarramundi Bridge would go under long before the dam waters would reach Richmond, but the far higher Richmond Bridge would be cut as the dam waters rolled over the local flooding. The Lowlands would disappear and the water would push up little valleys and roads, besieging Richmond, then carving the suburb into little islands. There was no way to stop it.

He could see part of Richmond Bridge through the swirling curtain of rain, and it was losing its battle already. The sandstone piers that normally looked like castles in the river were now no more than low boats, kicking spray high over the bridge. Cars were driving carefully over the bridge but there was a police car parked at one end with the blue light flashing.

Barney had a sudden wild thought: Just say you took your yellow canoe down from the hill and carried it to Richmond Bridge and launched it, now, tonight.

Barney felt a quiver of furtive excitement, the sort of feeling he had before he stood on Kelly at a canter, before he leaped from one tall fir tree to another. He almost felt warm.

Now that would be a great ride, past the farms and the caravan parks, past Colo River—maybe hitting the Hawkesbury with a metre-high surge like last time—spinning past Wiseman's Ferry and into the huge sandstone gorges of the lower Hawkesbury River. Under the long Brooklyn bridges, battling the wild storm in the long estuary, past Pittwater, past Lion Island and you are in the Pacific Ocean. Time to stop. All you'd have to do was stay right side up and the river would do it all for you. Tell that one to Mick and he'd go green . .

Tell that one to Mick and he'd throttle you. He'd tell Dad and they'd both put an axe through the canoe. Dad and Mum, they'd take turns in lecturing you till your ears dropped off.

But just say . . .

Barney squinted at the Lowlands again.

"Oh," he said softly. The glow of Barney's imagination died in the cold wash of reality.

The land was being slowly covered by water. The road had disappeared. The paddocks were little more than brown lakes with tussocks and wire. In the time Barney had stood on the hump land had quietly become water. The flood had started.

This was it, the limit. Barney decided that he should think of quitting. It was fine to think of riding a mad river in flood, but this was getting serious.

"Cuddles!" he shouted, a last nod to duty. He began to shuffle back down the little hill.

A frightened bleat. Something like a sheep with laryngitis.

Barney stopped.

The calf was standing shin deep in an open paddock less than a hundred metres away, alone, forlorn and totally lost.

"Okay, I'm coming," Barney said in a strange mix of relief and anxiety.

He waded into the paddock.

10

Pam held out the phone like a dead fish. "See? No sound at all."

Marge took the phone and jiggled the cradle. "Hello? Hello!" she shouted into the mouthpiece. "It's dead."

"Yes. What do I do now?"

"Maybe they'll fix it soon."

"Oh, fine. And while they're fixing it the Yarramundi Bridge gets flooded."

"You *could* stay here, like I said."

Pam looked at Marge.

Well? It's a simple choice isn't it? You go out and get wet and cold or you stay here and stay warm and dry—and bored. You can get bored anywhere. And you get to meet the Dracula lady.

"Will your mum mind?" The A-Team would be impressed.

"No. She's all right. You can share my room if you like. Come on, have a look."

Marge was bouncing to her feet. She led Pam down a dark corridor, past a small, paint-speckled mirror to a door plastered with animal transfers and whale slogans.

"Do you help the whales?" Pam asked.

"I write letters, but they never get printed."

"My Dad donates money to Bangladesh every year."

Marge swung the door open and ushered Pam in.

A room not much wider than the corridor. Bunk beds of white pine, the top headed with books and stacked clothes, a hand-made mobile of silver shapes clattering softly beneath a light, a drawerless dressing table. A small table with more books and a hard wooden chair, a music stand by the narrow window, a poster of a baby seal on a wall of old striped wallpaper.

This was a dump.

But there was something there, something from long ago.

Marge looked at her uncertainly. "It's a bit of a mess, but it won't take a minute to clean up. You can have the bottom bunk, if you want . . ."

The chair, perhaps, or the mobile or everything. Everything jammed in a tiny box of a room. Once upon a time you knew this. Something like this. Before Dad became A Success and the family had to move and move again. Before you started to put on armour . . .

"You don't have sisters, or anything?" For something to say.

"Nope. Just me. You?"

"You're lucky. Got a spoilt little brat, Stephanie. Makes all the noise in the world, all the time."

Stephanie came along after the move to the second house. It was like you lost your old friends, the ones you grew up with, when you lost that first

024572

1507

Valid only for Shell Pudsey Bear Mug Promotion.

May be exchanged for Pudsey Bear Mugs at any participating Shell Station in the U.K. provided that the correct number of vouchers is submitted. Details are contained in the Full Rules Poster and displayed at participating Shell Stations. Valid only while stocks last of any item or until the promotion closure date at participating Shell Stations of 31st December 1991.

1507

SR/127/91

024572

PUDSEY BEAR

MUGS

ONE VOUCHER

Redemption
value 0.001p*

Shell U.K. Limited

BBC CHILDREN IN NEED

SHELL SUPPORTS BBC
CHILDREN IN NEED 1991

020346

93 63 57 462 9

8192

1507

Valid only for Shell Pudsey Bear Mug Promotion.

May be exchanged for Pudsey Bear Mugs at any participating Shell Station in the U.K. provided that the correct number of vouchers is submitted. Details are contained in the Full Rules Poster and displayed at participating Shell Stations. Valid only while stocks last of any item or until the promotion closure date at participating Shell Stations of 31st December 1991.

1507

020346

SR/127/91

PUDSEY BEAR

MUGS

ONE VOUCHER

Redemption
value 0.001p

Shell U.K. Limited

SHELL SUPPORTS BBC
CHILDREN IN NEED 1991

house. But never mind, with the new house you got a brand new sister. Wonderful. Now there's the third house, the house above the river, and with this one there's a pony . . .

"It sounds great," said Marge. "This place, it's so quiet you hear the ants charging up the wall."

"Now that does sound great. Practising your music alone with no din."

Marge frowned at the recorder in her hand. She had forgotten that she was carrying it. "I only play this. I want to get a flute, when we can afford it . . ." She let the sentence die. "I hear you have a piano, even."

Pam allowed herself a smile. Yes, it is different now. Much better. "An old Gors-Hallmann upright. It's got a lovely tone. I'm on Grade Four now. Dad keeps on talking about getting a grand, but I don't know where we'll put it. And I don't know if I want it."

"Why on earth not?"

"Ah, even now whenever Dad has a party he wants me to play something from Mozart. With a grand he'd set me up with a candelabrum and a spotlight."

"You don't like that?"

"Would you?"

"Never in a million years. But, maybe for a grand, or even a Gors-Hallmann, I might put up with it."

Pam retreated from the tiny bedroom and shrugged.

"You have a lot of parties?"

Pam sighed. "It's part of Dad's job. A lot of business gets done at Dad's parties."

"He must be important."

"Oh, he is. Very important."

"But the parties, they don't sound like much fun. Not for people that you like."

"That's silly. We like everybody." Pam swung from Marge and walked away down the corridor. "Anyway, what does your dad do, Marge?"

Marge hesitated as she followed Pam. "Was a manager," she said quickly.

Pam stopped in the kitchen, looked about at the old yellowing fridge, the painted wood cupboards, the stained and dripping tap, the peeling ceiling. "Manager?" she said.

"He doesn't live here any more."

"Oh."

"Ah, that's history. We're getting on all right."

"Must be hard, though, what with your mum's allergy."

"Allergy, what allergy?"

"Isn't she allergic to the sun?"

"Allergic to the—where'd you get that? Oh, yes, the A-Team strikes again. Bunch of silly girls spending all their time making up rumours."

"Hey!" Pam stepped back as if struck. "What, because we won't let you in?"

"Oh yes. Sure. And you're not with them either."

"I am!"

"No you're not. You're a guest. They latched onto you when you came to Richmond, when you were lonely, to see what they could get out of you. But it won't last."

"Why not?"

"Because you're not dumb enough. They won't

allow you to stay unless you're dumber than Annabel, and that is *real* dumb."

Pam felt like laughing. "*You* think the A-Team is dumb?"

"Doesn't everyone? Look, sorry, it's your business. I just don't think you're one of them."

The curl of a smile died on Pam's lips as she realized that Marge was not attacking her at all. "Well, why does your mum only go out at night?"

"She's out now."

"Well, nearly only at night."

"What does your mum do?"

"Nothing much. Keeps house, fixes parties, plays tennis . . . Why?"

"Well mine works. In a job. At night. Annabel or somebody must be seeing Mum going to work in the evening, or coming home in the early morning."

"My mum used to be a secretary."

"Mum is a night nurse."

"Oh." Pam blinked. Trying to remember something.

"Yes. And she goes by Morris Minor, not by broomstick."

"In hospital?"

Marge paused. "No. In private homes."

Pam looked at Marge and began to nod. "I knew one . . ."

Marge was watching Pam's eyes. "What's wrong?"

"I had a grandma once." Pam was stumbling over her words. "Very sick. This nurse stayed with her for weeks and weeks . . ."

"Yes?" Very gently.

71

"Until she—Grandma—until she died."

"I'm sorry."

"Your mum, she like that?"

Marge looked away. "Sometimes. It happens."

Pam suddenly pulled a smile from the shadows. "Ah, doesn't matter, long time ago. Don't know why I thought of it."

Marge smiled back. "Well, do you want a hot shower, a change into something clean, warm and dry?"

"Well . . ."

"We can get the heater going and watch—"

"I don't think I can stay, Marge."

Marge stopped, let all expression wash from her face, and waited. The lemon gum creaked and thrashed in the wind.

Pam's eyes darted about, hunting for a way out. "The parents."

"Yes?"

"I wasn't thinking. They don't know where I am. They'll be frantic."

"They know you're out of the rain, safe in a house."

"That won't be good enough. You don't know Mum. She'll be phoning the police all night. I've got to go."

Marge raised her head at the sound of a car turning into the drive. "It's Mum. *My* Mum. She'll know what to do."

Pam shifted. "Maybe she can take me home . . ."

"Maybe." Marge stepped toward the door.

And Pam heard a heavy crack and a long sucking sound under the quiet throb of the approaching car.

She frowned as Marge's eyes widened. Then

Marge began to run.

The sucking suddenly became a wet tearing of the earth, a sighing into the wind and a crash, immense enough to shake the house as if it were a kennel. Heavy timber snapped, metal shrieked, clanged and somebody screamed briefly. Marge hurled the back door open and skittered down the steps. Pam started after her, then turned and ran through the lounge to the front window.

The lemon gum was down, wrenched from the soil and flung across the lawn and through a shattered fence. A white car, an old Morris, was pinned to the ground by the trunk of the gum. The starred windscreen peered over the trunk at the wreckage that had been the bonnet and engine. The two front wheels staggered apart in total surrender.

The passenger door swung open and a hand thrust out from the bottom of the opening door, splashing down on the lawn. Marge ran up to the car and stood there, water running down her slick of hair and her open mouth. A woman's head pushed past the door, low down and she began to heave herself out of the car. Air hissed from a tyre and the car settled under the weight.

Pam ran back into the kitchen, snatched up her raincoat, dodged across the lounge again and opened the front door. She reached the car as Marge helped a woman in nurse's uniform to her feet and she held the raincoat over them while the mother limped to the open door. They stopped under the slight shelter of the house eaves and turned back to see the windscreen crack, then shatter as the gum rolled slightly.

"Are you all right, Mum?" Marge was shouting

over the drumming on the roof.

Mrs Hamilton swayed a little and looked down at a stockinged foot. She was dripping heavily on her carefully cleaned rose carpet. Then she laughed. "Oh, apart from being nearly killed by our pet tree, I'm fine, dear. Wonderful."

"You see?"

Mrs Hamilton took a tiny step forward and a tiny step back and swayed again.

Marge swooped to her side and caught her elbow.

Mrs Hamilton twitched a smile. "Just a little woozy. Who's your friend?"

"Pam—Pamela Browning."

"Hello, Mrs Hamilton." But Pam was already pulling on her raincoat.

"This is her first year at Richmond. She lives over the Yarramundi Bridge."

Mrs Hamilton jerked her head up and seemed to be trying to look at Pam. "You shouldn't be here, dear. I'm dripping everywhere."

"The phone's been cut," Marge said.

Mrs Hamilton nodded aimlessly as if she was not listening at all. "You go and get me a cup of tea, Marge. I think I'll just sit down for a minute or so." She collapsed on the couch.

Marge tried to say something, gave it up and bustled into the kitchen.

"Pleased to meet you, Pam. It's nice when Marjorie brings some of her friends home."

Something in the car buckled loudly.

"Oh . . . the car is being wrecked completely! I don't know whether the insurance covers this. It happened so suddenly. But you should be home before the floods really set in."

"Yes, I—"

"I would take you home but—yes—my car is broken down . . ." She panted for a few seconds. "That was frightening. Perhaps if we phoned for a taxi or something . . ."

"The phone is broken down, too, Mrs Hamilton."

"Oh, I see . . ." Mrs Hamilton was sinking into the couch, looking like a washed rag doll. "Perhaps you had better stay . . ."

"But it is all right, Mrs Hamilton. My Dad will pick me up down the road. I'd better get there. Good bye Mrs Hamilton, 'bye Marge."

Pam rammed her hat on her head and hurried from the house before anyone could think of stopping her.

11

For a long moment nothing moved. Darcy leaned
far back on the bike and stared through the glistening rain and the glare of the van's lights. The
cowboy stood beside the van, blowing steam into
the rain, eyes glittering in the black shadow of the
hat. Darcy could not stop panting.

He's been hunting you all that time. Since you
snatched the bike. Went home, got that scrapheap,
that's what he did. Just drove around, looking and
waiting. What is he going to do now . . . ?

The cowboy gripped the door with a massive
hand and slammed it with enough force to rock the
van. He was carrying something that gleamed in
his other hand.

Darcy twitched the throttle in a moment of
fright. The bike roared and jumped forward. He
felt the front wheel lift from the ground and he was
doing something, moving, on the run again.

He rolled the throttle all the way back, felt the
back wheel buck and skid under him. He kicked
himself up and away from the saddle. The cowboy
stopped and looked up at the rearing machine the

boy had flung at him. Darcy landed in the mud, turned and leapt at the fence. For a long time he was scrambling on the boards, clawing at the splinters, kicking for a foothold, hearing only his own terrible panting.

But he reached the top without being plucked down like a fat chicken in a fowlhouse. He threw a leg over the side and looked back. The cowboy had fallen back against the wall and was wrestling with the handlebars of the bike, arching away from the still spinning front wheel. Darcy raised his hand to wave a mocking farewell—and the cowboy hurled the bike aside as if it was a kid's tricycle. Darcy dropped his hand and rolled over the top of the fence.

He landed in a small yard and was running before he realized he had thrown himself into a trap. He was bolting toward an old brick wall a few metres ahead, with a small door that looked as if it had never been opened. He was splashing down a starved and drowned garden with an apricot tree leaning against a high stone wall. On the other side of the garden a rusted fire escape climbed a blackened brick building, with the lowest step standing over three metres from the ground.

He had jumped from an open box into a closed box and the cowboy was heaving himself up the fence behind him.

What does he want? He's got his bike. Isn't that enough?

Darcy reached the door and pulled, pushed, kicked at it. It was as solid as the brick wall.

Wants to drag you off to Sergeant Henderson, so what? No . . .

"Kid!" The cowboy was propped on his arms on top of the fence. The rain was battering the hat into a rag, dissolving the shirt covering the thick muscles, changing the man into a gorilla.

Wants something to hit. Like Pop. Worse than Pop.

Darcy went up the apricot tree like a hunted possum. He stopped when a branch began to bend under his weight and the cowboy gripped the tree and shook it.

"Whaddyou want?" Darcy shouted. The sound of his voice horrified him. A squeak like a girl.

The man shook the tree again, then stepped back and kicked it. Darcy could feel that kick through the branch he was gripping.

"You!" the man shouted back. Just the one word, before he started climbing.

Darcy inched further along the branch and heard a quick snap. The branch dipped, forcing him to jump up and out across the neglected garden, toward the rusty fire escape. He seized a vertical bar and a handrail, which bent under his fingers. His feet swung under the landing, then back, searching for a foothold.

The cowboy stepped from the tree and walked under the fire escape. He reached up and almost touched Darcy's trailing foot. Darcy yelped, hooked his knee on the grid, kicked his toe between the two lower bars, straightened his legs, ignored the pain and slithered onto the grid of the landing. His knee was bleeding, his legs and arms tingled from many scratches, he was as sodden as a dishmop, he was panting so hard his ribs ached and he clung to the bars like a monkey in a cage, but he was safe.

"I know you, kid!" the cowboy shouted.

Darcy stared at him through the grid.

"All m'life I been knowing you, kid. You're the kid that grabs bags from old ladies and kills calves and ducks. You gotta have your fun, no matter what, just so long as you don't have to pay."

Darcy shook his head.

"But this time it's different, kid."

Darcy squeezed the bars.

"Time to pay."

Darcy pulled himself to his feet. He knew he was up here and the cowboy was down there and there was no way from there to here, but he could not steady his hands. He did not know he could feel as frightened as this. Even at home.

"Hey," he called, a little faintly.

The cowboy was walking back to the fence. "Yeah, kid?"

"I only borrowed the trail-bike. That's all."

"Today."

"What?"

"What about yesterday in m'calving paddock or last week shooting at the water tank?"

"Hey, hey, I never been near you before."

"Sure."

"Honest. Ask anyone . . ."

"It don't matter, kid. You lousy kids are all alike. You do the same things everywhere and say the same things. You're just the one I've got."

And he charged across the small garden stamped and jumped. His fingers locked on the grid, his body flattened on the underside of the grid and his legs rose above the landing.

Darcy kicked at a leg and the cowboy twisted and dropped to the ground.

"Right," said the cowboy, felt his knee and walked back to the fence.

Darcy tried the door in desperation, set his hands on the fire escape rails and tried to kick the door down. The door remained firm, the rail came away in his hands, dumping him on his back on the landing grid. And suddenly he was no longer frightened. He was angry.

The cowboy loped across the garden, soared to the bottom bar, writhed his legs in the air and pulled himself in jerks and spasms toward the top bar. His right hand clamped the top rail and he grinned at Darcy as he raised his body.

Darcy uncoiled from a corner of the grid and slashed down with the broken rail. The cowboy had just enough time to whip his hand away before the broken rail hit the metal with a ringing clang. He fell to the mud and watched the boy go berserk in his high cage. Darcy slashed about with his broken rail, hitting the bars, the grill, the iron door, the brick wall, fighting an army of ghosts.

The cowboy stood in the mud and backed slowly away.

Darcy stopped swinging. "Hey!" He clouted a bar. "Hey mister, hey gorilla-head! I'm not one of your kids and they're not me."

The cowboy raised his arm and threatened with a finger.

"I'm bloody Darcy Harris, all right?"

The cowboy looked at Darcy for a while. "Okay, Darcy boy, the cops can have you."

He climbed over the fence.

12

Barney made a loop from bailers' twine as he approached the calf with a comforting smile fixed across his face.

The calf bleated at him and moved further into the paddock. It did not trust the smile.

"Cuddles? Come on." Barney offered an open hand and slipped forward quietly.

Cuddles leaned back but sniffed in the direction of Barney's hand.

"Good girl. Come on, and we'll get you dry and warm . . ." He stumbled into a hole and splashed desperately toward the calf.

Cuddles reared out of the water and twisted away with a hoarse bleat. Barney turned his stagger into a heavy run and caught Cuddles by the tail. Cuddles bellowed and tried to gallop through the water, her eyes wide and staring, the mouth curled back. Barney was pulled to his knees as his grip slid to the tip of the tail. He pushed a foot under him and leapt for a hind leg. Cuddles kicked at him, then propped, legs stiff and apart as Barney slid up beside her.

"It's okay now, Cuddles. Really okay." Barney spoke softly into the calf's right ear as he adjusted the loop of bailers' twine in his hand. He shifted his lock on the calf's neck and eased the loop over her nose.

"Easy Cuddles, easy . . ."

The sky cracked over their heads. The detonation in the clouds made Barney duck and he knew what the sound was; the calf did not. Cuddles screamed in panic, thrust her head into Barney's loop and bolted. Barney was yanked off his feet, to his knees, to his belly, kicking like a landed fish. He was kicked above his left ear, blinded by flying mud and hauled into dark deep water.

He could not breathe.

Something tugged at his shoulder and snagged him. The bailers' twine burned his hands. He let go.

He still could not breathe. There was nothing to stand on and something was holding him down.

For a moment Barney wanted to shout in the water, kick out at anything he could find. Then he remembered that he was supposed to be a good swimmer. Hell, he was! That trophy—the one Mick filled with lizards and things—told him that. He wasn't going to drown, was he?

Keep it cool.

He reached for his shoulder.

Wire. Barbed wire. A lot of it.

That calf's gone and dragged you into a trap. Fine, so you can swim, but you can't swim out of barbed wire. Nobody can!

He opened his eyes, misty black, and began to thrash his arms.

Stop, stop. You can do *anything* kid. You can ride a horse standing up, go waterskiing down the Hawkesbury, start Dad's tractor, do geometry. There is nothing you cannot do. So do it.

Barney watched a large bubble drift past his nose and closed his eyes. He picked at the barbs at his shoulder, felt a slight rip and he was drifting free. Just like that. He could feel his knees dragging on ground, then his elbow banging on something hard. He raised his head and felt the rain beating on his cheeks, heard the rumbling of the storm. He coughed and gasped until the cold terror let go.

The calf. Where's the calf?

Barney pushed himself from the mud, kicked a boot loose from a strand of wire and stood. Muddy water gushed down the inside of his raincoat. His hat had gone. He seemed to be standing on the edge of a flooded waterhole near a wire fence, with shallow water swirling across the paddocks. But there was no sign of the calf.

A thrashing in the water. Across the waterhole, near the fence. One skinny black leg, another.

Barney pushed himself around the depths of the waterhole, tried to run. Couldn't. Boots were full of water, sucked at by the mud. Could only slog toward the calf.

There was a tangle of wire in the way, spreading from Cuddles like an ugly flower. Barney hesitated, then strode forward. He pressed against the wire, reached out for the calf's nearest hind leg and pulled. He could see the calf's head rising slowly toward the surface, the mouth gaping open, the eyes swollen, fixed and staring.

Dead?

Cuddles kicked against Barney's hands. And the head broke water. And gasped.

"Got you."

And stopped. The calf's body was held back by three strands of rusty barbed wire, one across the neck, two across the belly. Barney was not only heaving on a heavy, struggling calf, but also the unseen dead weight which was pulling it back into the water. Cuddles roared in pain and twisted in Barney's hands. The head dipped back into the water and Barney lost what was left of his grip.

"Oh Jesus," he whispered.

He blundered forward and groped through the muddy water for the calf's body, the neck, slipping the wire over the head.

"It's okay, fella. We'll get you out . . ."

Cuddles surged from the water, bellowing hoarsely, trying to gallop onto Barney's back. Barney fell, felt the hooves briefly on his shoulder and wires whipping at his back. He sat neck-deep in the water and watched Cuddles kicking down a singing snarl of wire, pulling a rotten post from the bottom of the waterhole.

"Cuddles . . ."

The calf half-turned, kicked at the post and disappeared beneath the water again.

Barney blundered to his feet and saw that Cuddles was thrashing underwater with her legs locked around the post and the wires winding around her body. He caught the neck, went down with it and braced his legs in the mud. He tried to straighten, to lift the head above the water. That was all.

The dark water funnelled down his neck, flowed

over his shoulder, bubbled in his ear. The calf was bucking, squirming, fighting him.

"Sorry, sorry, you've got to come . . ." He heard a strangled sob in his voice and bit back his words.

The thrashing slowed.

Barney rolled desperately from the calf and grabbed at the post. He shook his head and heaved. The muscles at the base of his spine bunched, his legs quivered and it moved. One of Cuddles' ears touched the surface for a moment.

Then a fresh current of muddy water buffeted Barney, raising the water level by the length of a hand and Barney could not hold his effort. He looked down at the calf. The calf looked up at him and an explosion of air escaped from its mouth. The smell of warm milk washed across his face for a moment, then it was gone. The rear left leg moved feebly across Barney's leg and sank.

Barney threw himself against the post for a final, total effort and this time he could not make it move. He sagged away from the calf and the post and felt the muscles of his back throb and radiate pain.

He brought his hands to his eyes and his body began to shake.

13

Pam stepped up onto the trunk of the fallen tree and stayed for a moment. A single spike of wood pointed at the sky from the base of the tree, but everything else was torn away and flattened. There was no space between the crumpled car and the ground and there seemed to be no more than a handspan of crushed metal under the trunk. She shrugged, stepped down and walked fast out to the road. Just in case Marge and her mother would try to call her back. But she heard no cry. Nobody ran after her. They were probably still staring at the wreck and had not noticed that she had gone. That was fine. The wreck was all their problem, wasn't it? Theirs and the State Emergency Services, when they got around to it. Getting across the Yarramundi Bridge was her problem.

She started skirting puddles to keep her feet dry, but the puddles were flowing into each other and finally the road became a canal, its surface etched by the wind. She stopped, made a face and paddled through the water.

It was cold and she would probably walk into a

row now, missing the bus, getting home late, wearing somebody else's dress and wet shoes. She didn't care.

She stepped into a pot-hole and stumbled a few steps.

And socks. But what are you going to do now?

Walk home.

In this?

It's only a bit wet and windy.

Oh yes. And you are going to walk across Yarramundi Bridge?

The bus crossed it a little while ago.

That was nearly an hour ago. The river is rising all the time.

Perhaps I should have stayed with Marge.

And how dare she! Calling me lonely. Me? I've got all the friends in the world.

Pam saw the grey cubicle of a distant phone booth and walked toward it, as the sleeting rain drove her inside herself. She felt the cold muddy wash about her feet, the constant sting on her cheeks, but she began to forget about it.

No wonder the A-Team had shied away from Marge. She was bad news. She was dull. Annabel can't even do her Dracula Lady bit now. That's the end of the leer and the horrible cackle; that's a pity. I mean Annabel and Therese are great doing their thing. They really destroyed Graham's address to the school with a touch of Groucho only yesterday. Perhaps you don't tell them that the Dracula Lady is only a nurse.

A nurse like Gran's . . .

And Jan could do something too. Brilliantly, whatever it was. She did Marge bumbling about with a hockey stick so well you had to fall over laughing. Jan had Marge's lonely, hurt expression down pat. She threw it back at Marge once and Marge did not know what was going on. Marge never knows what's going on. But it wasn't a case of picking on Marge. The A-Team has a go at everyone.

Marge doesn't like us. Along with all the dummies who call us the Trendies. Well, fine, we don't like them either.

But where were the A-Team when Uli's gang started the attack?

That's different. You deserved it, opening your big mouth to Rader like that. They were mad at you, but it won't last. They're your friends, and you'll get together again. Spend whole nights in each other's places. You can even smoke and drink wine at Annabel's place. The parents don't care.

Annabel, Violet, they were on the Yarramundi bus. Why didn't they stop it?

Pam was pushed to a stop by the wind and she heard the howling, the metallic hum of the swaying electric lines. A loose iron sheet flogged a leaning wall. She ducked and shuffled on.

Doesn't matter. They are friends. Marge has no friends, no proper friends. You have to pity her.

But you don't have to stay with her.

Except she wanted you to. And she helped. Stopped you burning down the school and everything . . .

She was walking on a twilight slope, with scudding shadows and not a trace of colour. The houses with their cascading roofs, the bent trees with their billowing foliage, the fast rolling clouds, the rain, the road, the spreading water—everything was grey.

You can still go back.

No.

Why not?

You know. Have to get home.

Why?

Because Dad and Mum, they don't know where you are, and they worry.

Do they?

Of course, look at Mum on the phone, just about falling apart. And Dad? Remember when you fell off that itty-bitty cliff and Dad raced you to hospital with his hand on the horn all the way. For a bruise on the shoulder. It was so embarrassing.

They'd be more worried if they knew where you are now.

I'm safe, now. Wet and cold and everything, but safe. And I'm going to phone them in this phone box.

And if you get through?

Then they can work it out. They always do.

And if you don't get through?

Shutup.

Pam reached the phone box and swung the door aside. She stepped inside and stood dripping for more than a minute, feeling her cheeks burning. She wiped her face with a damp handkerchief before lifting the receiver. It purred hopefully.

What are they going to ask you to do?

Nothing. Just stay here and Dad will be here in five minutes. Nothing, no miserable flood is going to stop the Brownings.

But there was a time, long ago, when the

Brownings were not fighting the whole world . . .

Pam frowned and shook her head. She dialled the number and heard a low hiss, as if there was a tired snake on the line. She banged the receiver down and tried again. The snake sounded a little angry.

All right, what are you going to do?

She looked at the steamed windows with their frantic rivers rushing down the glass. She felt as if she was sitting on the bottom of a wild sea. She did not want to go back into that.

You know you should go back, don't you?

Back to Marge's?

What's the real reason for you being out here?

Don't know what you mean.

It's the house, isn't it?

Oh come on.

Nothing like Braeside, the house on the river hill, is it? Nothing like the sunken lounge and the dark slate floor and the walnut table and your bright plastic study with your own TV set. No, Marge lives in an old house, with worn carpet, flyspeck lights and chipped crockery . . .

But your first house was like that.

And Marge's mother, with that terrible job.

And Mum used to stagger off a train and collapse on a couch and talk for hours about the office where she worked. Stupid bosses counting paperclips and losing fortunes, girls talking all day, and her getting more and more work. Her job must have been the worst in the world, the way she talked. Then Dad saved her. Different house and she didn't have to work any more, just look after the house and baby Stephanie and play tennis. But she didn't talk much now.

90

There's Marge's dad, gone and she looked sad, like she wanted sympathy. Why? Fathers are there or they're not there, doesn't matter either way. I mean, when did you have a long talk with Dad? Never, that's when and he's there. So Marge's dad is not there, so he's not dead, just somewhere else. That's not tragic is it? 'Course without Marge's dad there's not much money about.

But Dad says people get what they deserve and maybe Marge and her mum don't deserve much. Oh, we send money to Bangladesh because Dad says the floods are not their fault, but most times it is people's fault. Dad leans on the walnut table and says we have a nice house and everything because we work hard—even mum hostessing—do smart things and don't make mistakes. Most people make mistakes . . .

That's what Annabel says.

The kids around the first house, they always made mistakes. They didn't care. Come last in a race, and what does it matter? Girls playing cowboys, wearing second-hand clothes—even mouldy sports tunics—what does it matter? It matters in a lovely Braeside and around the A-Team. There you have to put on armour.

Pam stared at the rain exploding on the phone-booth glass.

At the time of the first house there was no armour. No need. Dumb kids playing Monsters and screaming like idiots and Gran mixing a cauldron of lemonade . . .

A confusion of images tumbled in from the storm. The walnut table, polished and alone at Braeside, Marge's mother staggering from her car in her rumpled grey uniform, Gran smiling at her with unbelievable innocence. She—a bright little girl, now—was holding a cluster of bright cards over the walnut table and shouting, 'You're cheating!' and Gran was laughing at her. 'Old ladies are allowed to cheat,' and Gran won her fifth Happy Families game. It was all right, the loser's slice of cake was always far bigger than the winner's. And most of the time they were out of Gran's house exploring the beach, collecting wondrous shells and talking about the monsters and the maidens under the sea.

But then Gran was lying in bed, fading to a shadow on the sheets, and a warm woman in a nurse's uniform was reading a book gently to her. The woman picked Pam up, held her close enough to draw a slow smile of recognition from Gran, and read on. Just once the night nurse looked up and watched Dad with contempt in her eyes. Dad wasn't with Gran; he was looking around the cottage and running his fingers carefully over the walnut table. It was the last time Pam saw Gran.

Pam jerked her head up and pushed at the door of the phone box. The rain swirled in around her legs. She stepped out into the storm and walked along the empty road to Yarramundi Bridge.

14

Darcy stopped under the dying cherry tree outside his home and humped his shoulders. Nothing had changed, nothing ever would unless some lardhead went and burned it down. Which wasn't a bad idea. The shack—you couldn't call it anything else—was high on a bare hill, leaning toward the spreading river and wearing its rust red roof like a tipped cap. The door was open, it was *always* open because half the shack had sagged a few years ago and the door wouldn't close any more. Grass grew through the rotting verandah planks; a pile of empty beer cans fought the strangling weeds and the once-white curtains threshed against the streaked windows, the only sign of life in the shack.

But of course there was Pop. Still sprawled in one corner of the verandah, and some of the rain must be curling in to reach him. Not that he would be feeling anything this late in the afternoon. His six-pack, his latest six-pack, was down to two.

On other days, better days, Darcy would think of heaving a stone onto the corrugated roof over Pop's head and watching him fall out of his chair.

Just to remind him of the .22. Sometimes Pop would forget to get him back. But this time he was in trouble, so bad it sat in his belly, nibbling, and would not go away. This time Pop might start acting like a dad and come out of the fog long enough to tell him what to do.

Darcy moved toward the shack and a blue light flickered in the front window. So Ma was home, as always. But perhaps she could help.

He stepped onto the verandah and dripped heavily on the boards.

Pop glared at him with hooded eyes. "Bit wet."

"They sent us home." He was shivering. He knew that was because he was soaked to the bone, and cold, but also because he was frightened. He knew the feeling, like when Graham had called Ma up to school, or when he was still little and there was a gang looking for him. But this was far worse. He had started something and he couldn't stop it.

"Saw the school bus going past. Hours ago. What happened?"

"Bit of trouble." Darcy scraped a shoe on the edge of the verandah. Maybe it would be better to change into dry clothes and then talk about it.

"You burn the school down?"

"No . . ." Kicking mud from the boards.

"Who's that?" Ma, sounding tired and slightly alarmed. Maybe it would be better to talk it out with her. There was a time, when Pop was gone when they were sort of mates . . .

"Your kid. Lousy wet."

"Oh . . ." And she went back to the TV.

"Whatcha do, then?"

Darcy looked up. Get it over with. "Borrowed a bike."

Pop looked wearily at the can he held in his hand and slowly crushed it. "Borrowed?"

"Took."

"A bike?"

"Trail bike."

Pop looked at him with a gleam of interest. "Where is it?"

Darcy suddenly realized that Pop had been sitting on the verandah, curdling, since he lost the BSA. If he had brought the Yamaha home, Pop would have taken it and ridden it over the hills until he fell off. He would have grinned at Darcy, treating him like a war mate, making jokes, telling him how they would battle the lousy world together. Until tomorrow.

"Lost it." Darcy shrugged.

"What d'you mean, 'lost it'? Couldn't you ride it?"

"Ah Pop, you shoulda seen me going through Rickaby's Creek, a roarin' great river. Was doing wheelies, the lot. Pretty well jumped a van."

"What was the van doing?"

"Trying to catch me."

"How come? How'd he know you were on a nicked bike?"

Darcy stood on the verandah and dripped on the rotting boards.

"Prob'ly nicked it on the main street, eh?"

Darcy jerked his head up.

"You did? You really did? You nicked an old bush bike from the main haul before every lardhead in Richmond."

"Whatsit?" Ma caught the rising voice and creaked on the couch.

"What a great gink you gotta be! Why the bloody hell did you do it?"

Darcy groped for a defence. "Thought you'd be sorta proud . . ."

"Proud?"

"'Cause you taught me, Pop."

"Taught you to be a stupid thief?"

"Like when you nicked me rifle for grog."

Pop sat in silence for a moment, his face becoming dark and mottled, then he hurled the crumpled can at Darcy's head and hit the corrugated iron roof.

"Whatsit?"

"And I gave it to you kid, don't you forget that. Maybe I just didn't think you were worth it."

"Just because I'm not one of your crummy mates!"

"Don't you ever sling off at my mates. Better than you'll ever be . . ." Pop's anger died a little, to be replaced with a touch of sadness. "Like Splinter, breaking through the ambush with two bullets in his hide . . ."

Darcy turned off. He had heard Pop's Vietnam stories many times, knowing them all by every worn line. There was no stopping Pop once he had started, all you could do was wait around until he had run down. Darcy could vaguely remember how it was in the beginning, when he wasn't home and Ma would talk about him as if he was a general with medals all over his chest.

". . . listening to the trees creak . . ."

They had a brick house then. Then Pop came

back, a bitter man with nightmares and a violent temper. Ma stopped talking about her general; Pop started losing jobs and started talking about what lousy things the government was doing to him.

". . . we could smell the blood in the APC for months . . ."

For a while Pop brought his war to Richmond. Oh, one night he came back with a .22 rifle 'for his kid' and for maybe a week he wanted to make him into something like one of his war mates. Then he dropped the idea. Never knew why. He brought cars to the back of the house—different cars every week—and the garage began to fill with strange things, vacuum cleaners, cases, filing cabinets, copper pipes. Then Sergeant Henderson—no, he was a constable then—came round and Pop disappeared for a while and home became the falling-down shack. When Pop came back he mostly fought his war in the shack. Drank his dole money, pinched and sold the rifle and punched and kicked and slept through the day.

". . . watching the mildew grow . . ."

Pop would remember his old battles a lot. He would remember the one battle he could talk about, never the other battles he would remember when he had finished with the beer and slid into sleep. The battles he could see when he moaned, muttered and, just sometimes, screamed.

"But maybe it's all right. Greatest mates a man can ever have, and you don't forget that."

But you never see them, Pop. They never come and see you and you never try to find out where they are. Maybe they don't exist.

"Come home, lose the mates for a wingeing

woman and a kid who thinks he's showing guts by nicking a toy bike on his way home. And losing it. Hell. I shouldn't have named you after a great Aussie fighter, kid. I shoulda called you Tiny Tim."

Darcy swallowed. He was silent for a moment and when he spoke his voice was cracking. "Anyway, I don't lay about all day for the dole!"

Pop swung a loose hand at Darcy's head and clipped his nose. "Watch it, fellah. And it's a pension, from the government, thanking me for what I done for the country."

"Yeah, sure."

"For what the country done to me."

"Whatsit?" Ma stood in the doorway, shaking a little. She looked at Darcy with slightly glazed eyes, her stained floral dress was askew and her tangled brown hair tumbled over one eye.

"Go away, Else." Pop flicked his hand at her, dismissing her like a fly.

"What's wrong, Darcy?" Ma ignored her husband and even tried a smile for her son.

"Ah, he always picks on me."

"Not worth the trouble."

Ma combed her hair with her fingers and swept it back from her face. "You're wet," she said. "How'd you get so wet?"

Darcy saw a fresh bruise under her right eye. "It's raining, Ma. Look at it."

"Where's your raincoat?"

"Prob'ly the cops have it, eh?" Pop said.

"Police?" Panic swept across Ma's face. "What have you done?"

"Stole a bike." Dad laughed suddenly. "We get

to see Henderson again. Lucky us."

Ma looked at Darcy as if she expected the wound. "Had to happen, didn't it, Darcy? In jail now. But you won't break my heart again. No. There's nothing left."

"But the cops may not come here." Darcy was wishing he hadn't told anyone about the bike. He wanted to go away, far away, for a long time.

"The police don't know who stole the bike, then?" Ma looked up in fragile hope.

"Don't think—"

"Where is the bicycle? We must get rid of it, throw it in the river."

"It's a trail bike."

"He lost it."

"Lost it? The police have it? What about fingerprints?"

"No, the cops never got it. Maybe they don't know about it. Maybe they'll never know." Clutching at straws.

"Who's got it?" Pop slowly got to his feet.

"I'm wet all over . . ."

"Oh. Let him change, Norman."

"Who's bloody got it?"

"Ah, the stupid farmer I took it from."

Pop took a small step forward, then one back and he sat down again. And laughed.

"What's so funny?"

"Some thief you are, boy! Pinch something from someone, but that's all right, because this is the thief people pinch things back from!"

"What was I supposed to do? Stop him?"

"Oh no, no. Did you see him, then?"

"Ah yeah. Big farmer, mean."

"Did he see you?"

"Yeah."

"Close up?"

"He just about caught me."

"So all you had to do, really, was give him your name."

"Oh yeah. Ha ha—" And Darcy stopped and remembered himself shouting at the cowboy from the fire escape. Shouting his name.

"Oh man," Pop said. "He did. He really did. Go and make some tea, Love. Sergeant Henderson will be along in a minute."

Pop rolled back on his seat, closed his eyes and laughed until he wept.

Darcy spun from Ma, from Pop, from the shack, and ran back into the storm.

15

Barney waded across the big paddock without knowing where he was going. He felt numb, as though he had lost a vital part of him. He felt the pull of the rising current on his legs, the flattening wind on his side, but he was only seeing the calf. Staring at him, through the rushing water, the last tiny bubbles seeping from its mouth.

Asking for help, Barney thought blackly. Pleading. Dumb animal, probably thought I could save it, lift it from the flood and take it home to Mum. Why not? I'm one of the super creatures that somehow get hay for it, sit about on those metal monsters and run the world. You'd think that this super creature could do something about things this time. But no. Mick could, he would have pulled the wire apart; Dad would have worked out some way to make the flood pull the calf out and even Mum would have done something. She'd have seen the wave in time to do something about it.

But Cuddles, you were real unlucky. You got found by the one person who just couldn't do anything at all.

Why did I have to find her?

After a while Barney realized that he was no longer pushing through the swirling water, but that he was raising his heavy boots for each step. He was climbing. He turned in dull surprise to see that he had left the flooding Lowlands behind him. The wire was invisible, he could not find the calf now. It was maybe three fence-lines away. He could not remember climbing any of those fences but he must have to get where he was. He could not remember moving from the flood but he was still carrying the flood in his boots.

He sat on a hummock and raised his legs, one by one, allowing the cold brown water to sluice over his legs and belly. He was too wet to care. He stood again, squelched his toes in his socks and leant against the wind. He noticed that the raincoat was torn in several places and that his hands were bleeding but he had not been feeling them.

He supposed he should go home. It was getting to that time when Mick would be expecting him to be coming back. But then what? 'Did you find the calf, Barney?' 'Yes, I found it.' 'Where's the calf, Barney?' And then you have to tell them all about it, how you had your hands on that calf and how it went and got drowned in your hands and you couldn't do anything about it.

No, you don't want to go home yet. Not until you have had a little time to think things out. Just a little bit of time.

Barney climbed the hill to the lower road, turned away from his home and walked across the low hills north of Richmond. The sky before him rippled and blazed with unseen lightning and the hills were given a ghastly glow. Richmond was another planet and Barney wanted that feeling, even the rain and the wind flogging his face. If it continued for long enough, the image of Cuddles drowning might drip from his head.

He tried to remember a worse time than this, and failed. There was Aunt Sarah, who had died in a car accident two years ago. He had liked her, with her tinkling earrings and her fantastic travel stories, but he had only seen her a few times and when he had been told about the accident it seemed a long way away. As if it had happened to someone else. There was the concussion, the time he had gone skiing with Mick and hit a tree. He could see two Micks waving across each other as they bent down, but the pain was never that bad. And Mick had been almost touching in his care for his little brother, had terrorised him for a month to reset the normal balance. No, that was all right, it was just the normal sort of thing, and there was none of this guilt thing. There was the time you borrowed—all right, stole, Mick's bush knife and lost it . . .

Barney stopped as he saw someone walking his hills, a woman, a girl, coming down from the highway. He did not want to share the hills with anyone now. He wanted to walk in the rain in his own little world until he was too tired to think of his calf.

But he *knew* the girl, and maybe he needed help to change the terrible image in his head.

"Pam!" he called.

The girl continued to walk fast, possibly faster.

Barney squelched rapidly toward her, waving as

he walked. "It's all right, Pam! It's me, Barney!"

Pam kept her pace for a few steps, then reluctantly allowed him to catch up. "Barney." She looked at his face and hands and her face changed but she did not comment. "I'm in a terrible hurry."

"That's okay. I'm going your way. You walk how you like."

"Oh, all right." She swung off down the road.

"Where are you going?"

"Yarramundi. The bridge."

"Oh." Barney faltered and Pam surged ahead for a moment. "Why're you going there?"

"I live there. On the other side."

"Oh. Yes, that's right." And then Barney understood what had been said. "But you won't get across there now."

"Who says?"

"I've just come from the Lowlands. I—uh—It's beginning to go under."

Pam shook her head. She wasn't going to be stopped by anything. "Maybe the bridge is higher."

"The bridge is lower than just about anything. Never tried to cross the bridge in a flood."

"The bus got across."

"When, just now?"

"Pretty well. Look, you leave me alone, Barney. I didn't ask you along."

Stupid heifer, thought Barney, and stopped. He would go home and forget about the girl. She could get herself drowned—

No. Not again.

He caught up with her. "Look, I've just lost a calf." The road crossed the Yarramundi Billabong, almost a low bridge over flowing black water.

Pam glanced at the water and slapped quickly along the gleaming bitumen. "So go and find it."

"It drowned."

Pam stopped. "Oh. I'm sorry."

"Doesn't matter. It's just the flood is not funny any more."

"The calf. It drowned on the Lowlands?"

"Yes."

"You saw it?"

Barney felt something in his throat. He nodded and gestured with his open hands.

"You're bleeding. In the face too. Did the calf fight?"

Barney wiped the back of his hand on his forehead. "Tangled in wire." He realized he should not have mentioned that the moment he said it.

Pam nodded to the low crest between her and the river. "Look, I'll just have a look, okay? See what it looks like. If it looks at all dangerous I won't try it."

Barney hung his head and sighed. "Okay," he said.

Barney followed Pam up the curve of the road, past the blossom tree, the open iron shed with its tractor and cultivator, past the small sealed white house . . .

Pam stopped. "Oh," she said.

16

The road was barred by two orange and black trestle-barriers with winking lights. Beyond the barrier the road curved down into blackness and lightning glimmered on moving water ahead.

"They put the barriers up too soon. Bet the bridge is still high and dry." Pam hesitated, then slipped between the trestles.

Barney shrugged and followed her. "How do you know?" He sounded impressed.

"Dad says the people that work for the government, the police, the council people always go the easy way."

"Oh."

"The person who put the barrier up probably did it the moment the bus passed so he could have a cup of tea somewhere . . ."

Barney stopped, and did not say a word.

The bridge was gone, as if it had never been. Pam had walked from the shadow of the cutting into a broad panorama in black. Streams raced from their feet to the muddy car park beside the road and on into the river, hissing softly, fast and now almost a hundred metres wide. The road had become the river and the ends of the bridge were marked by a few signs standing in the river. This side was marked by a high rectangle of black diagonal stripes; a depth gauge showed the river was flowing 0.8 of a metre above where the bridge had been, and a large sign mocked drivers by forbidding them from overtaking on the bridge. On the other side a battery of signs faced away, now a little island in the middle of a sea. The river scudded past a yellow speed limit sign, too far away to read, and a pair of trestle barrier lights sat on a low hill, a dry sentry.

"It's gone." she said, her voice dead.

"No. It's there. Just." Barney was staring at the water, staring *through* the water, as if it frightened him.

Pam frowned and turned back to the river. Yes, the bridge was still there, if you looked. There was a long straight hump, no higher than an open hand, running most of the way across the river. She thought she could see the edge of the bridge just below the surface. If Yarramundi had rails like any other bridge she could climb across without getting her feet wet. But Yarramundi had no rails, just boot-high wooden sleepers marking the edge. You could hit those sleepers with a bike on a fine day and topple down into the river.

Pam walked toward the edge of the river.

"What are you doing?" Barney hurried after her, caught her by the arm.

"Just looking." Pam twisted free. She stopped a metre from the river and watched two pines swaying in the river. Normally they would be standing on islands downstream from the bridge, now they were slowly being drowned.

"You're too close. Come away." Barney lurched into the barrier. He reached for her again and missed.

Pam cocked her head and looked back at him. "Are you frightened?" She was surprised.

Barney looked away, at the black rushing water. "Yes," he said simply and bleakly.

"That's silly. It's there. We're here. What can it do?" Then she remembered the tree being destroyed by wind and water.

"It's not funny, Pam. You should be scared too. If you had a brain in your head."

"Thank you, Barney."

"Come on. Let's go!"

Pam took a step toward the curling edge of the flood.

"Come on!" A shout with an edge of panic.

Pam could see the edge of the bridge now. Streams of small bubbles were flushing through the holes built in the sleeper-sides to cope with an overflow. The holes were useless now. And if she looked very hard she could see the old diagonal planks of the bridge, the worn studs that held them in place. Not much more than shin-deep, but the water was streaming over the planks as fast as a bolting pony.

"Ah, come back, Pam. Please." He was trying a new tactic. Not like him at all.

She smiled at him in the glimmering light. "I'm safe, Barney. Look, dry feet."

"You're not safe! It comes in waves, could be all over you."

Pam clicked her tongue and thought of a reply, but it died on her lips.

A gust came down the river, holding a fistful of birds. It swept a slanting curtain of spray up from the river, flattened a brace of trees on the other side and spun Pam back into the barrier. It shrieked, deafening Pam, forcing her mouth open. She was falling, but slowly, bringing the end of the barrier up into the air. She felt stunned, as if she was being pushed from her body, and she watched the birds. The birds—maybe ibis—were trying to fly, but the gust was tossing them about like balls, banging them together, scudding them on their backs. For a moment a grey bird rode the wind, held its wings at an angle and soared toward the dark sky.

Then the gust plucked it from the air, swept it down to the other tumbled birds, and hurled them all into the flood. Pam thought she heard a desperate cry, but she couldn't see any of the birds again.

"You all right?" Barney was pulling her upright and the wind had softened again.

She nodded. But she wasn't. Suddenly she understood about Barney and his calf.

"Come on. Get away from the river."

There was something terrible in the air, something reaching out. Before today, death was a moment on television, a remote moment in a movie or in a strange country. You kept it remote by sending money and not thinking about it. But it had gone wrong today. You go to a girl's home and her mother spends her nights touching it. You go to a rainswept phone box and there is a painful old memory waiting for you. You meet a boy you know very well and he has it on his hands. And then you see it. A gust swirls past and a dozen die. How close can it come?

She nodded again and allowed Barney to lead her away from the river.

"You can't go home, now. What are you going to do?"

She shrugged. She supposed she could go back to Marge and apologise and everything.

"Well . . ." Barney looked embarrassed. "Well, I suppose you could come home with me."

"Oh." She blinked at him. "Won't your parents mind?"

"Nah. Not tonight. And Dad'll work out some way of telling your parents where you are. He's good at that sort of thing."

"Well, thanks. But how are you going to fit me in?"

"No worries. We can put you in the barn, with all the cows."

"Oh, fine."

"Hey, I was only joking."

"I don't care. I'm too wet, and tired and everything." And maybe you don't want to see Dad. Just for tonight.

Barney turned to walk up to the top of the hill. And stopped. "Ah, no," he said.

Darcy Harris was barrelling down the hill.

17

Darcy kicked along the black road in white fury. He did not know where he was going and he did not care. He just wanted to get away from that dirty little shack, and his weepy, hopeless mum, and Him. For ever. For as long as he lived. As far as he could go.

He had nearly hit Dad this time. Nearly swung his fists into him. And maybe it would have been hard enough to stop him from swinging back. Oh, he'd hated Dad almost forever, just didn't know how much. But even Dad knows now.

How much anger do you store away every time he finds your hoarded coins and spends them on a flagon of sherry? The rage comes, burns through you and goes, but every time there is a speck of anger that stays, for the next time. For when you take him a report card full of fails and he calls you an idiot and heaves it at your head. Or won't let you help service the BSA because you're stupid. Then *he's* the one that goes to jail. For when she begs for food money and fails, and he hits her for not feeding him properly. For when you learn to

111

love that .22, clean it, oil it, wrap it in rags, learn to snap a top-notch pigeon from the sky—and one afternoon it's gone and he's laughing.

But this was more than that. Even that. This was when you got into black trouble that you couldn't get out of. For the first time. This was the time he—and even she—should've tried to see what they could do to help. Backed you up—you're their kid, aren't you? But no, he had to have a shot, make it a laugh show . . .

Darcy slowed when he saw the Yarramundi Billabong lapping at the road, and realized he had been striding out for the river. A brief, thin smile washed across his face and increased his pace.

Okay Laughing Pop, Graham, Rader, all the kids who think I'm a bone with a punch, Henderson, who's always been waiting, Mum-who-sits-and-takes-pills-and-pretends-she's-not-there. Well, it's my turn. I'm not going to be here any more.

I don't need you. Any of you.

Darcy began to climb the hill.

When Henderson gets to our place and gets funny about which one of us he wants this time I won't be there to hear it. I'm going to be across the river and so far away they'll never find me. Shooting crocodiles in the Territory, maybe, or game fishing off Cairns, or working a freighter to Rio. I'm big enough, now. I'm tough enough. Nothing's going to stop me . . .

Darcy kicked his way through the barrier and saw the two figures standing near the glistening sea.

Every time, he thought. Every bloody time you want to do something there's something jammed in your way. So, what did you expect?

Darcy kicked mud at the river.

The bigger of the two people at the barrier raised a hand.

Not cops. That was something. Too small for cops. So what were they doing here?

"Hi, Darcy," Barney called over the wind.

And that silly bird Pamela. Her here? Barney, you'd almost expect. He'd be chasing birds or horses or something so he could be covered in mud and muck. But Pam, she should be watching TV, or organising a pyjama party, or dancing jazz or something. But she's not doing any of that now, is she? 'Course she lives across the river. Could be waiting for Daddy in his silver jetboat . . .

Darcy walked slowly down the road toward the river, hands in his pockets, leaning hard into the wind.

"You're wet," said Barney.

Darcy looked down at his school sweater and his trousers, blackened by mud and water, clinging to his body, pouring a dozen cataracts onto his shoes. "Lost the coat," he said. "Doesn't matter. What you doing?"

Barney looked at Pam. "Ah, just looking at the river."

Darcy rubbed his nose. "Hey, you live over there, doncha, Pam?"

Pam seemed to flush. "Yes." She thought a moment. "But I'm staying here, on this side tonight."

"Yeah, well . . ."

"I am staying with Barney's family." With a strange touch of defiance.

113

"Can't go over there tonight." Barney watched a fat swell curl down the river and over the bridge. The river spread out over the road as the swell passed, but it didn't go down again.

"Richmond Bridge is probably still above water." Darcy started to measure distances and times. Half an hour, maybe, and he'd be on Richmond Bridge.

"I couldn't get home from there," Pam said, huddling her neck in her raincoat.

Darcy turned to walk away. "Yeah, well . . ."

"Ah, it'll be under any minute now," Barney said. "For sure the cops are there, stopping people."

Darcy turned back. "You reckon?" And he didn't have so much as a five cent coin in his pocket. Where're you going, Lardhead? Maybe, just maybe, Pop, everyone, is right about you. Stupid.

"For sure. Look Pam, we've got to be going."

"There's someone on the other side." Pam pointed at the stained flare of stationary headlights, reflecting in the surging water.

"He's not going far tonight," Barney said.

"Or maybe for two weeks." Darcy laughed, feeling a slight lifting of his frustration. At least he had someone to share it with.

"It's Dad," Pam said uncertainly.

"Ah, get out, yer can't see anything but lights."

"No . . ." For one moment Pam seemed to be reluctant, then the relief flooded into her face. "It's Dad! I know those lights. The two big beams, far apart, and the left parking light is always winking. See?" She jumped up and down and waved her hands.

Barney looked at the lights and across at Pam with worry in his eyes. "Hey, don't."

Pam ignored him. "Hey, Dad! Dad!" she shouted into the wind.

"Stop it, Pam!" Barney caught her arm and pulled her down and into him.

"Let go of me, Barney Stevens!" Pam struggled.

"He might think you're calling him on. Stop it Pam!"

"Go away!"

And then Darcy looked at Pam fighting with Barney and saw it as if from the other side of the river, from the always hostile adult mind, as he had been trained to do by a hundred ugly encounters.

"Stevens! Get away from her!" He chopped at Barney's arm and Barney turned with pain and surprise on his face. "He's going to think you're attacking her!"

Barney looked across the river and his face changed. He dropped his arm and stepped back from Pam.

"What did you do that for?"

"He's coming," Darcy said flatly.

18

Pam saw in Darcy's face a deep-set dread, something she'd seen in his face when the headmaster strode toward him with his lips pressed white, but far worse now. She looked across the river and saw the lights retreating rapidly from the barrier on the other side.

"He's going," she said and felt a little disappointed. She glanced at the boys and they were both looking grim, expecting something else.

The lights stopped half-way round the bend and charged down on the river. They swayed a moment and the barrier skidded across the road and toppled. The lights glimmered a second as the flood erupted before them, and the Range Rover seemed to be sinking like a thrown stone in the river.

"Ah Gees . . ." Barney breathed the words. Pam was not sure she'd heard them.

No, the Rover was not sinking. The water thrown into the air by the splash was being swept away by the wind and there was a low bow wave gurgling at the base of the headlights. Dad was going to make it. Dad always makes it, like a knight on a charger galloping to rescue his best daughter, his 'Princess', from the terrors of the flood.

"What a twit," said Darcy. Almost spitting it out.

"Hey, that's my father."

"Yeah."

Barney wasn't saying anything. Just staring at the lights in the river.

All right, they were jealous. They wouldn't fight this flood or anything else, so they hated someone who would. That was the difference. Dad had once saved a kid from a rip. He told us about it a few times, said you could tackle the worst thing around if you knew how to do it. Dad knew how to drive across a flood and Barney and Darcy didn't know anything about it. Like the rip, easy if you use it like an escalator to get you to the kid and then swim across it to get out. Simple, Dad said.

Barney took the flickering light from the barrier and walked to the edge of the flood. He stood in the centre of the road and swayed it from side to side. And the Rover kept on coming.

It was the same with business. That's why we don't live in a scungy house in a scungy street near a factory any more. Like he said, see what needs to be done, and do it.

That why we have the walnut table?

"There's two people in that car . . ." Barney held his free hand over his eyes.

Sheet lightning greyed the black sky behind the Rover, picking out the square shape of its cabin and the two heads in the cabin. One big, an adult, behind the wheel, the other only high enough to appear a hump in the passenger side.

"Stephanie . . ." Pam said and felt Darcy's eyes fixed on her face. "I don't know *why*." She stared at the head of her little sister.

But the Rover was nearly across. You could see the foam of the dark water pushing on the side of the body, tilting it on its springs until one headlight was almost submerged. You could see the frightened eyes of little Stephanie, Dad's white hands on the wheel. The Rover was only fifteen metres from the edge of the flood. You could hear the engine roaring through the wind.

Barney stepped back to let the Rover past, pulling Darcy as he moved. Darcy shook him off but walked off the road.

Pam stared at the Rover, wanted to cheer but was suddenly struck by the terror of getting into the Rover and going back into the flood.

Then the engine of the Rover died.

19

Barney watched the bow wave roll from the grille of the Rover and die. He could see two wide-open eyes just above the dashboard as the shadowed man's lips jerked.

"What are they doing? What?" Pam hissed in his ear.

The man was leaning over the wheel. The starter motor cranked and the light beams dimmed and trembled.

He won't start the engine now, Barney thought. Not now, with all that water pushing into the engine box. What can he do?

The starter motor turned a little slower. Then the man stopped a moment and turned the lights off. Barney thought he could hear the whimper of a little girl over the surge of the flood and the wind. The man looked up at the sky, as if he was whispering a prayer, and turned the key again. But the starter motor was dying now, slowing with every failed attempt.

"It's no good," Barney said to himself.

Pam looked at Barney with sudden slitted eyes,

as if he had caused all this.

The passenger-side headlight, the downstream light, was almost underwater but the driver-side light was rearing clear of the water. The river was pressing at the side of the Rover, flowing whitely round the shining wheels, surging angrily over the mudguard and the bumper, trying to lift the Rover and hurl it from the bridge. As Barney watched the Rover moved.

"Oh God . . ." Pam shuffled from side to side, then she spun away and ran up the hill, away from the river.

Barney watched her go in confusion. He looked at Darcy and Darcy's face was alight with some slight triumph, as if he had known everything that had happened would happen and he was just going to watch it all.

On the bridge the Rover squealed and lurched sideways. The man grabbed the little girl from her seat and leant against his door with her face pressed against his, as if her added weight would keep the Rover's wheels down on the planks. He was shouting at them, white-faced and desperate, but Barney could not hear anything that made sense over the storm.

The man had to do something, very quickly, before the flood got under the Rover and began to lift. No, *they* had to do something; there was no way around it.

The man was pushing with his shoulder and the length of his body to force the door open against the rushing current. The door nudged clear of the side and shuddered wide open with the man shouting and river pouring into the cabin.

"They're gonna drown," said Darcy.

The man relaxed a little and the door slammed like a pistol shot. He squirmed in the cabin behind the little girl and wound the window down. He shoved his head out of the window and shouted at Barney, "Give us a hand, kid, eh?"

Barney looked across at Darcy.

Darcy shook his head. "Ah no, Stevens, you're not getting me into that. That's his worry."

And Barney stared at the ten metres of glistening black water between his feet and the heeling Rover. Water running so fast it etched lines in the light that hit it. It hissed at him as it curled away from the road and swirled into the angry depths.

Barney suddenly realized that he wanted to run away, to run away like Pam, to pretend he had seen nothing. Perhaps he could run all the way to the phone box on the hill and call the police. It would be too late. The police would never get here in time, but he would have done something. He would have the excuse.

The Rover shifted, skidding a little on the timber of the bridge.

"What's he want us to do?" Darcy said. "Fly?"

But that was it. Nobody expects Darcy Harris to do anything. He's never done anything in his life. Everyone expects Barney Stevens to do something now. Dad, Mum, Mick, Mr Graham, they all look on you as the star athlete, school captain, top kid. It's been good, this feeling of trust—take the tractor down to Mick, son, look after the cricket equipment, Barney—but it's no good now. If you do nothing now nobody will say anything. But they will all look at you a little bit differently. Even

121

Mum.

"Yeah," Barney said. "They all want you to fly."

He put a foot into the water and felt the power in it, scudding across the rubber, punching at the foot, building a wave and breaking into spray. He could see the calf's eye in the water now, and he could remember what it had been like minutes before, being tumbled across the paddock, helpless, with mud and water being forced up his nose. He had never been so frightened. Until this moment.

"For Christ's sake, help us!" The man was holding the little girl out of the window, and the child had her eyes closed and was screaming.

"The stupid—" Darcy's words were snatched from his mouth by the wind, but it didn't matter.

Barney took a deep breath and stepped out into the flood. His leg was immediately clutched by the flow and pushed slowly aside. He took a wide step to strengthen the grip of his first step and felt himself being spread like a wishbone.

It was too powerful. He had always known it would be. It was much too powerful. He was like those ibis in the wind, already helpless and doomed.

Another step. A small one but he was already moving not to the Rover but to the edge of the bridge. He had to go back. But they were watching, the stupid father of Pam's and the little girl. Another step. Darcy was right. Pam's old man had got himself into this, let him get himself out. But what about the little girl?

Stephanie had stopped screaming now. She had been half withdrawn into the cabin and she was staring at Barney.

Perhaps a tiny little shuffle against the current, to get away from the bridge.

"Come on, boy," the man was calling.

Shutup.

"Come on, son, not far to go."

Barney looked up and felt his foot slide. He tried to move his other foot downstream to save himself, but he was falling and there was nothing he could do to stop it. He thrust his hands down to hold his body from the water, but his arms were swept away, twigs in the flood.

He was down, rolling, water rushing under his coat, seizing him like a glove, scraping him across the bridge and now the bridge was gone and there was nothing but water . . .

20

Pam ran off the road to the small white house on the top of the hill, shouting before she reached the door.

"Help us! Help!" But there was no light in the house. She hammered on the door with the flat of her fists, tried to turn the knob, stepped back, slapped her hands together several times and ran to the open shed beside the house.

There's nobody here, nobody. It's always like this. We always have to look after ourselves. The boys won't help. Nobody helps. They'll just stand in the rain and watch . . .

She skidded into a rusty tractor, opened her mouth to shout again and heard the constant din of water exploding on the corrugated iron roof, like someone hammering in her head.

God, Step's face . . . Little monkey, trying to stand up and play the piano with her teddy . . . Without Step that house would be quiet as a tomb.

Shut up!

She had to do something. Like Dad said, you can do anything if you get your mind to it. But what,

what? The tractor. Drive the tractor down to the river and pull Dad's 4WD to safety.

Pam stepped up on one of the massive treads and peered at the controls. There was no key.

Of course you can't drive it. What were you thinking of? Find something else. Quickly. Step shouldn't be there, should be home wrecking the piano . . .

The curved plates of a disc plough gleamed in the half-dark, marching away from her.

It'd be like Gran. So empty. No, worse than Gran. Bundle of whooping giggles, it can't happen.

A heavy draft-horse harness hung on a rusty hook. A pile of oat bags sat on a palette and leaned against a wall. Heavy rope coiled on a sawn-off beam. A bucket of nails . . . The rope, the rope!

Pam flung herself at the beam, wrenched the rope from it and staggered back to the tractor. It was *so* heavy. She pushed herself upright and lurched into the rain. This time the wind was on her side, pushing at her back, keeping her almost running despite the weight in her arms. She reached the road in a few seconds and began striding down the road, the knotted end of the rope bouncing after her.

It was all right. She was in time.

The lightning shimmer played on the white roof and bonnet of the 4WD, showing that it was still on the bridge. Dad was leaning out of the passenger seat with something in his arms and some dark figure was just standing there—Darcy Harris, of course. Well it didn't matter now. She would get the rope down there and throw it to Dad and that would be that. Perhaps . . .

Something in the water between Darcy and the 4WD. Didn't see it before. In a yellow raincoat. Boy. Barney. Almost there. Dad shouting at him. Probably telling him to go back, don't be silly . . .

Oh!

Barney stumbling in the water, falling, being swept away by the black river.

Pam stopped. "Do something!" she screamed.

21

Darcy had no intention of moving when Barney toppled into the river. He was watching the boy stepping nervously into the wild water and thinking of what a stupid situation this was getting to be; that he might stay around and watch Sergeant Henderson try to rescue Pam's stupid dad, her yowling baby sister and good ol' Barney. Because that was how it was going to end up, for sure.

And then Barney was down in the water and Darcy was nodding.

See, Stevens, you can't beat them. Ever.

Darcy kicked at the river in a moment of rage. A kick, a step and he was up to his knees in the water, snatching Barney from the river like he snatched the Kawasaki from the cowboy. Just making his anger felt.

He suddenly became aware of what he was doing, and where, as Barney came into his right hand, and for a moment he stopped. He looked around, half-expecting Uli's mob and Pop to be standing on the bank, laughing at him, then the river pulled Barney from him. He pulled back, and

Barney was the Queen Mary tugging him into the river, down to his knees and off the bridge.

Black water streaming, swirling everywhere. He let go of Barney to reach for air and something round banged hard into his back. He began to feel very angry. Barney grabbed at him. He hit Barney, rolled over Barney many times, felt Barney slipping away and grabbed him like a log. His free hand hit a root or a branch. He clutched at it and the river poured down his neck. He gasped, growled, found a foothold and heaved Barney out of the river into a straggly bush.

The river launched a heavy branch at his hip. It hurt, but not enough to dislodge him. He growled, shouldered clear of the water and surged up the bank. He dragged Barney through the undergrowth back to the road and left him, coughing. Pam's father was still shouting.

He suddenly coughed deeply, shuddering the length of his back, and he could taste the foul water of the river. He propped himself on his knees and sucked air. He could see Pam running toward him, her mouth open. Didn't she scream at him before? Now she was screaming at him but there was only the wind howling into his ears. And her Dad was shouting at him. Pop was shouting at him, all the time. Henderson, the cowboy, the teachers, Mum, they were all shouting at him. They never stopped shouting at him.

And that bloody river was stopping him from breaking out, getting away from them all . . .

Darcy kicked at the river and skidded, half-fell to the road, grazing the palm of his left hand. Barney panted beside him, looked at him as if he was

trying to work out what it was all about, and began
to show the beginning of a smile.

Just too much . . .

Darcy jerked himself to his feet and roared at the
river—the thing that was locking him in like a cage,
like a prison, was pouring into his nose, was clinging to him in his long-sodden clothes. Making him
a fool, a lardhead.

No! Bloody no!

For an instant Darcy saw Pam's dad appealing to
him with one hand and the 4WD was moving, then
he was running across the road, gaining speed with
every swinging stride. Then he had veered left,
kicking savagely at the river at his feet, defying the
claws of the rushing water to hold him. He shouted
at the river, fighting it as if it was a man, like a
cowboy, like Graham, like Pop.

The river chopped at his legs, wobbled him,
slowed him, turned him. He hit the 4WD on the
side of the right mudguard and draped over it like a
flung sheet. Pam's dad was yelling at him.

"You pushed me! You pushed me!" he said.

Darcy straightened his back against the wind and
he worked toward the cabin, his shins thrust painfully against the bottom of the 4WD. He found the
step under the water and stood on it. The 4WD
dipped back to near normal, but it was now a rock
in a torrent. The rear of the 4WD was angled
against the current and the left wheel was probably
being pushed hard against the sleeper rim of the
bridge.

Darcy stared at the man as he began to understand the situation. His anger was dissolving.

"That's good, kid," said Pam's Dad, as he tried

to quieten the child. "You saved that stupid boy and I'll see that people know about it. Maybe a medal, eh?"

Darcy was wondering what happened. Now he was stuck on a car in the middle of a flood with a right dribbler and a yowler and they were all going over the edge any minute. Really bright, that.

Pam's Dad smiled up at him hopefully, waiting.

Darcy saw Pam standing at the edge of the river with coiled rope hanging from her shoulder, and Barney sitting on the road, coughing. Nobody else. A gust of wind punched him in the back, sprawling him over the side of the 4WD. The 4WD lifted under the force of the wind.

"What—what do we do now, kid?" Pam's Dad talked very quickly.

"Dunno."

"I mean we've got to get going fast now. Eh? You can start the engine?"

The headlights were fading now, making Pam a shadowy ghost. "You got to be kidding, Pops."

"What are you going to do? Have you got a plan? You had to have *something!* Eh? Eh? Oh my God."

Pam took the rope off her shoulder, grabbed an end and threw the rest at Darcy.

"Oh. Yes, yes. Pamela will do it. Yes . . ."

The rope was caught in the air by the wind and whipped sideways to entangle itself in a tree. Pam's Dad pounded his fist on the wheel and Darcy felt the 4WD lift under his feet, almost floating in the current.

Any minute now, any second. And there is nothing to do. When it goes, you just hang on until we hit a tree or something.

130

The kid looked at Darcy in the flickering half-light and yowled.

"Hey, kid." Darcy sat on his voice and tried to sound calm. "You shut up."

"Hey!" Pam's Dad lifted an angry finger then let it fall. His daughter was quiet.

Pam pulled the last of the tangled rope from the tree as Barney dragged himself to his feet. Barney said something to Pam and took the rope from her.

There's a chance, just a chance.

Barney walked against the wind, upriver and off the road. He stopped, fiddled with the rope, leaned against the wind and did nothing.

"What's that fool boy doing?" Almost a shriek.

Should've taken the end of the rope from Pam. You didn't know she had it, did you? Should've waited to find out. But you couldn't make it here *with* the rope . . .

Barney hurled the rope, not to Darcy and the 4WD but into the teeth of the wind. The wind turned it and scudded it into the river. A poor failure.

Except that the river was uncoiling the rope as it swept downstream. It could pass close to the 4WD.

Darcy stepped into the flood again, shuffled forward and the rope was passing a metre away from the front bumper bar. Darcy leapt at the rope, caught it and leaned up and back. He grabbed the towing hook as his body banged against the bumper bar, pushed the rope round the towing hook and began to fight the river.

Most of the struggle was underwater. He put his shoe through a headlight in a moment of satisfaction and found the tyre with his other foot. He straightened his legs, passed slowly under the rope and forced himself up and over with the water exploding over his shoulders.

He pulled himself to his feet by reaching for the external mirror and pulling. He left the mirror warped and twisted, but he was standing and he could breathe. He gasped for a few seconds, would have made it a few minutes, a few hours, but Pam's Dad was shouting again.

"Get the rope here, kid. Quick, kid."

At least he wasn't complaining about the damage done to his lovely Rover.

Darcy pulled the rope from the hook, wound it twice round his waist and moved back to the cabin. He hauled an extra length from the river and passed it to Pam's Dad.

"Just hold it," he said.

"That boy. He shouldn't have taken it from Pamela. Pamela would have reached us properly next time. Don't you think?"

Darcy unwound the end from his waist and passed it round the steering column.

"Hey, I can do that. It's all right." Pam's Dad let the rope go and reached for the end.

Darcy felt the rope burn through his fingers. He grabbed at it, held and pulled it through the steering wheel and out of the 4WD. He would not trust the man to do anything any more. He tied a fast rough knot with a few hitches and waved at Barney and Pam on the road.

Barney pulled on the rope until it rose from the river, an arc pushed sideways by the wind. Barney was leaning way back but the rope was pulling him in a little shuffle toward the river. Pam looked behind her, picked up the end of the rope and took it round the trunk of an old pine. She pulled and Barney staggered back in surprise. He looked at Pam, nodded and worked his way toward her. Together they pulled the rope almost straight and knotted it.

The 4WD moved.

"What are they doing? What?" Pam's Dad shoved his head out of the window.

"Give me the kid."

"Eh?"

"Come on, Pops. We got no time." Darcy stepped into the flood, foaming at the knee. The side of the 4WD began to rise behind him.

Pam's Dad stared at his four-year-old daughter for a moment, then passed her out of the window. She wailed, kicked Darcy in the neck.

"Come on, Stephanie. You've got to go before the river gets us . . ."

Darcy hooked his arms around the rope and clamped his hands together on his belly. "Come on, Step. Is it Step? We're not going to get into the river. Promise. Give you a ride."

Pam's Dad pushed her out through the window, sat her on Darcy's neck and she didn't fight or wail this time.

"Now what you've got to do is stay up there. Hang on real tight. Okay, Step?"

"Yas." Stephanie locked her feet together under Darcy's jaw, grabbed his nose and his hair and rammed her chin onto his head. It hurt, but he had other things to worry about.

He shuffled sideways toward the safety of the road, small steps, tiny steps, with the water thrusting at his knees, the wind pushing him hard against the slope of the cabin.

"Hey, how bad is it, kid?"

Now the cabin was gone and the wind howled in his ears, trying to bend him backwards over the bonnet. He could see the silhouettes of Barney and Pam heaving away at the rope. Silhouettes? Silhouettes because the headlights of a car were coming down the hill behind them.

"What about me?"

Get nicked.

Now the bonnet was gone from behind him, the rope was giving way and he was slipping toward the edge of the bridge.

Blue light above the headlights.

Stephanie screaming in the storm, so scared. Her little fist slipping from his nose. Stopping, catching her hand, pulling her arm across his mouth, biting her sleeve and holding. There was really nothing but the battering of the wind, the roaring hiss of the water, the hard, stinging lines of driven rain and the flickering black sky. Just keep on shuffling.

Foot finding the sleeper edge of the bridge. That's all right, you can press against the flood. It is easier.

"Gonna make it, Step! Hang on."

Stephanie stopped wailing and tried to find shelter beside Darcy's head.

The rope was sagging!

Pam's Dad was on the rope too and the 4WD was lifting, almost drifting as you watched.

Darcy was stopped. He could no longer lean against the flood and the wind. He was standing straight with Stephanie around his neck and he could not take a step back to save himself. As Pam's Dad moved nearer to him the rope would stretch, arch out over the river, not the bridge.

"Get out of it!"

The man moved blindly from his car, eyes closed, head hunched.

Darcy unlocked his hands and pushed himself from the rope. It was like pushing back a truck on a steep hill. He took two steps and then he could not find timber under his foot. He was twisting into the river.

Except some yellow curtain was shifting about him and Stephanie was plucked from his neck. He found the sleeper and for a long time he hung out from the bridge with the river pouring over him. Then the yellow coat had returned and he was being pulled up and clear of the river.

He watched Sergeant Henderson go out on his cable for a third time for Pam's Dad, to be winched in quickly. A few seconds later the 4WD tilted and raced off in the river. The rope snapped like cotton thread.

Sergeant Henderson turned from the river and peered at Darcy.

And Darcy remembered the trouble he was in.

"Darcy Harris?" Sergeant Henderson said, with astonishment in his voice.

Darcy waited.

"Well, whaddayou know . . . ."

22

Barney sprawled on the soft sand and let the sun soak into his bones. He was half-asleep on a small island above the bridge, a week from the flood. Already he had to think hard to remember what it was like.

Now the cars were rippling over the bridge as they always had and the timber had finally stopped steaming in the sun. Men were still cutting up branches on the banks with chain saws, a quiet drone in the heavy air, but there was nothing left jammed between the posts. Barney looked at the copse of pines on the north bank, trees combed by the flood and left raked like a flight of spears. The worst sign of the flood, and even here bright green grass erupted at their roots. He could hear the lazy hum of insects on his island, the cluck of birds reclaiming their old territories, the murmur of the river rippling over the tumbled rocks. In another week there would be little sign of the flood remaining, only that copse of leaning trees.

But it had been big enough. Downriver a herd of horses were seen swimming desperately in the

Hawkesbury; all over Sydney roads had become rivers with abandoned cars standing in rows like pebbles; suburbs became islands, streets of houses disappeared; a train sank. Richmond houses had worn bright orange ribbons, marking families waiting to be evacuated. The Lowlands had become an inland sea, with only telegraph posts and chimneys thrusting from the brown water. And several people had been drowned.

But Barney had watched all this from the dry warmth of the farm. He had been flicked across the ear for returning so late—and in a police car—but that was about the end of his trouble. Mick had even treated him like a lunatic hero for trying to reach Pam's dad, though Mum had told him, "There's no heroes in this house, thank you," and that was that. He had seen the Rover banging against Richmond Bridge on TV, but it was being bent by the water before it finally disappeared. He had seen Darcy Harris on the same programme, mumbling, looking sideways, ready to run at any moment. And he had sympathized with him. But even the death of the calf had been filtered and become almost painless. Dad had taken a phone call as the flood became a river again. "How are you, Murray? Yeah, that's mine. Yeah, thanks." Hung up, said, "That was Murray Stalben. Found the calf. Going to bury it. How's your horse?"

Barney gazed at the river, watching the silver water twisting, bubbling over tumbled pebbles.

It was back to normal, now. School tomorrow, swimming in the afternoon, Mick talking about buying a speedboat, Mum borrowing Kelly for a bareback ride down to the Lowlands. Nothing's changed . . .

The water danced and shimmered before the bridge and Barney felt a long cold tremor deep in his back.

But it has, hasn't it? It has changed.

Barney lifted his eyes and noticed a single figure standing still on the bridge, looking down. Not at the water, but at the sleeper Barney knew carried the scar left by the Rover as it tipped into the river.

"Hey!" Barney sat up and waved his arms. "Hey, Darcy!"

Darcy turned and humped his shoulders. He stood on the planks while five cars slipped past, as if undecided, then lifted a hand and crossed the bridge.

"How's it going, Darce?" Barney offered a hand as Darcy paddled to the island.

Darcy slapped Barney's hand and squatted next to him. "What you mean?"

"You know, since the flood."

"Since the TV bit? Gees, that was so bad with that ratty reporter, making me a lardhead in front of the whole country. Shoulda hit him."

"You were all right. Anything changed since then?"

"Oh yeah. Changes, and they're all bad."

"Get out! You are a hero."

"I'll flatten the next lardhead that calls me that."

"Okay."

"Ah, it was all right for a coupla days. Mum all of a sudden cleans up a dress and waltzes up to Richmond to buy a packet of tea and be seen and talked to. But she has to drop everything at home because Pops is down on me like a ton of bricks, calls me 'The National Hero' keeps on laughing at me, knocks me about a bit. Mum and me, we have to stay clear of him all the time when he's on the grog now. Now I know why she's on the valium."

Barney broke a twig.

"And Henderson dragged me down to Vic Browley, the cowboy farmer I borrowed a bike off. And now I've got to work for free on his stinking farm until Henderson and Browley decide I've done enough. Maybe fifty years."

"Free? Why?"

"Said I borrowed his bike, didn't I?"

"Oh. Yeah."

"Well I get to ride his bike on his farm and he keeps on talking about paying me sometime, but he's a lardhead. Watches me all the time like I'm gonna rustle his herd. Ah no, beat it."

Pam was walking toward the Yarramundi Bridge from the hills of the north. She saw Barney, waved, recognized Darcy and came over.

"Hi," she said from the bank.

"Hi. Come over," said Barney.

"What you do that for?" muttered Darcy.

"She was there."

Pam looked down at her sandals, wrinkled her nose and paddled over to the island. "Whatcha doing?"

"Talking," said Darcy.

"About that night?" And she became grave.

"Mostly. Any changes?"

"What changes? Why should anyone change?"

"Nothing. Just wondered."

"Saw your great Dad," said Darcy.

"Oh."

"In Richmond. Ignored me. Like always."

"Sorry," Pam sighed and sat beside Darcy. "Well, thanks for what you did that night. Thank you both. For saving Step . . . and Dad."

Darcy looked surprised. "All right."

"It's not so good at home just now." Pam chopped at the sand. "Mum seems a bit mad at Dad all the time, and she won't let him take Step anywhere without her. And Dad is angry at everyone. He's after Sergeant Henderson for letting the Rover fall into the river."

"Beaut. And what about Darcy?"

"Gets the blame. Really. All of us are blamed for 'mucking about' on the river edge and causing him to come across the bridge. Everyone gets the blame, except him."

"Yeah. Figures." Darcy flung a pebble at the bridge.

"Sorry. Well, I've got to go." Pam got up, waved briefly at Darcy and Barney and walked unsteadily to the bank.

"See, Barn, nothing changes, nothing at all."

Barney looked at his old enemy and frowned. "Hey, Pam," he called. "Where are you going now?"

Pam tossed her hair. "Nowhere, Barney. Just to Marge's place." And she slapped her sandals loudly all the way to the bridge.

Darcy's right, Barney thought. Nothing changes. No one changes except me.

And he knew that for the rest of his life he would remember the calf looking at him from beneath the water and the grip of the wild river on the bridge, his black terror as he was carried away . . . He would hesitate before diving for fear of hitting a rock, stop riding Kelly standing up, think before climbing into a paddock with a wild bull. He would face every new task with the quiet niggling doubt about whether he would be able to do it. He had found out that he was mortal, that he could fail badly, that he could really die. He was adapting to a slightly altered way of life.

"She's not all that bad," Darcy said slowly. He had been watching Pam stride across the bridge, even raised a hand when she stopped a moment where the Rover had gone over and shrugged, open-handed, to him.

"Maybe she's better," Barney hauled himself back from the depths of the river.

"Her pop is a stupid lizard. He's wrong. We didn't put him on the bridge. He did. We got him off."

Darcy blinked, testing a new thought on the surface of his mind. "Everyone was wrong, the TV reporter, Mum, Henderson, everyone. It wasn't me that got Step out of the river. It was Pam. She went and found that rope. It was you, Barn. You got me into the bloody river and got the rope to me. It was us."

Barney smiled, but shook his head and pounded Darcy lightly on the shoulder. "But it was you, Darce, who went and did it."

Darcy looked at the quiet bridge and the rippling water beneath. A slow smile crept onto his face and stayed. "Yeah . . ." His voice carried a touch of awe. "How about that?"

About the Author

Allan Baillie was born in Scotland in 1943, but has lived in Australia since he was seven years old. On leaving school he worked as a journalist and travelled extensively.

He is the author of six highly acclaimed novels for children, and an award-winning picture book, *Drac and the Gremlin,* illustrated by Jane Tanner. Many of his novels have been shortlisted for the Australian Children's Book of the Year Award.

Allan Baillie now lives in Sydney with his wife and two children and writes full time.

Also by Allan Baillie

Megan's Star

The kids at school think Megan is strange, but she feels depressingly normal, with ordinary problems.

But when Megan hears a desperate cry for help that no one else can hear, extraordinary things start to happen. She finds a boy trapped in a ruined house. The boy, Kel, is strange. He has rare powers and he knows Megan has them too . . .

'Set in the 21st Century, *Megan's Star* is an interesting mix of science fiction and traditional adventure story. It reveals yet another layer of Allan Baillie's talent.'

Shortlisted for the 1989 Children's Book of the Year Award and the 1989 NSW Premier's Literary Award.

Books For Keeps

Eagle Island

What could be in the mysterious box which Col dives so desperately to recover from under the sea? Will the island, which Lew had felt was his own, ever be the same again?

Eagle Island is a gripping adventure story. When chance brings these two conflicting characters together on a lonely island on the Great Barrier Reef, their encounter turns into a deadly game of hide-and-seek.

Another unputdownable, racy thriller from this best-selling Australian author.